HINGE

Praise for the Book

Vandana Kohli eloquently analyses the causality and manifestation of mental disorder in Indian society through her deep understanding of social structures that create complex emotional and psychological conflict and distress. She explains how accepted tenets of normality can often unhinge us and yet, we have it in us to get back to equilibrium with a little help from friends and our own inner voices. A wonderfully thoughtful book for everyone to reflect upon.

—**Kiran Mazumdar-Shaw**,
Chairperson and Managing Director, Biocon

Mental and emotional health are among the biggest challenges we face today and in the foreseeable future. Vandana Kohli's *Hinge* addresses, simply and elegantly, the complex working of emotions, to better understand their cause and effect. The suggestions it offers are of value to make *Hinge* an engaging and enabling read.

—**Cyrus P. Mistry**,
Business Leader

Vandana Kohli's *Hinge* synthesizes the lessons from modern-day science with approaches from Indian philosophical thought to offer small ways in which we can make big improvement in our everyday, modern lives. It provides an insightful illustration of the benefits of simplifying our lives through a focus on meaningful choices. I believe *Hinge* to be a very thoughtful book, and found it refreshing.

—**Sheena S. Iyengar**,
S.T. Lee Professor of Business, Columbia Business School and Author of *The Art of Choosing*

Without mental health, there can be no true physical health, especially in an era of cathartic change and uncertainty. Despite growing awareness, mental health issues are still mostly ignored or considered peripheral in India. It is reassuring to find Vandana centre-staging an important subject with great sensitivity, purpose and awareness.

—**Sunil Kant Munjal**,
Author and Founder-Promoter, Hero Group

With stress and anxiety on the rise, Vandana Kohli's *Hinge* is a gentle nudge towards understanding the construct of emotions and the link between the inner and the outer world. Through resonating anecdotes from ordinary lives and empirical views from renowned experts, it kindly and patiently guides to help us understand important emotions and their effect on us.

—**Dr Lobsang Sangay**,
President, Central Tibetan Administration, Dharamsala

Vandana Kohli has written an important and timely book on what mental ill-health can look like and what can cause it, with thoughts around re-discovering a balance in life. Real-life stories from the Indian context bring the narrative to life whilst her research references add credibility and weight. Vandana's prose makes what might otherwise be a challenging topic engaging and relatable. Mental ill-health affects almost two billion people every year and this book will help us make sense of the causes and of the possible answers.

—**Chris Parsons**,
Chair, India Practice, Herbert Smith Freehills and
Mental Health Champion

HINGE
(RE)DISCOVERING EMOTIONAL AND MENTAL WELLNESS

VANDANA KOHLI

RUPA

First published by
Rupa Publications India Pvt. Ltd 2021
7/16, Ansari Road, Daryaganj
New Delhi 110002

Sales Centres:
Prayagraj Bengaluru Chennai
Hyderabad Jaipur Kathmandu
Kolkata Mumbai

Copyright © Vandana Kohli 2021

The views and opinions expressed in this book are the author's own and the facts are as reported by her which have been verified to the extent possible, and the publishers are not in any way liable for the same.

All rights reserved.
No part of this publication may be reproduced, transmitted, or stored in a retrieval system, in any form or by any means, electronic, mechanical, photocopying, recording or otherwise, without the prior permission of the publisher.

Events described in this book are based on real-world situations. However, the name, age, profession and place of residence of the subjects of the case studies, have been changed. Any resemblance to persons living or dead resulting from changes to names and identifying details is entirely coincidental and unintentional.

P-ISBN: 978-93-90547-71-5
E-ISBN: 978-93-90547-79-1

Seventh impression 2023

10 9 8 7

The moral right of the author has been asserted.

Printed in India

This book is sold subject to the condition that it shall not, by way of trade or otherwise, be lent, resold, hired out, or otherwise circulated, without the publisher's prior consent, in any form of binding or cover other than that in which it is published.

CONTENTS

Preface   ix

Normal
1. The Social Normal   3
2. The Gender Normal   22
3. The Sexual-Sensual Normal   34
4. Normal in Mind-Science   49

Unhinge
5. Trapped: The Depressive Abyss   59
6. Breach   72
7. Intrusion: Point and Plane   80
8. Stuck: In Anger   92
9. Blocked   106

Hinge
10. Logic   129
11. Body   137
12. Thought   150
13. Heart   166
14. Centre   188

Acknowledgements   202
Endnotes   203
Index   207

PREFACE

India is distinct. Many layers of time and civilization spanning millennia occur alongside, interacting with each other. One may spot a bullock cart next to a Bentley. So it is with mindsets. A spectrum exists, from the profoundly inclusive to the intensely limiting, within both old and new.

Mental health rides on how we *feel*. Our emotions, in turn, are shaped considerably by socio-cultural norms. Early environment is crucial to the cues we take for anger and indignation, love and fear. Of course, our physical attributes and gender also contribute to how we feel about ourselves—whether we are sure or tentative, at ease or not. These affect emotions and their circuits as well.

This collection of essays focuses on hinges of emotional and mental wellness. It explores how the inner may fragment and what may help (in addition to medication, wherever necessary) in making it whole, again.

Section I considers what is largely the ecosphere of 'normal'. Narratives are drawn from the middle strata of society, where the means of living are in place. The search is for factors which, within the scope of normal, could rouse disquiet in a person who may otherwise be well.

Section II probes social and psychological triggers to our emotions that cause inner strain and distress. It explores the power of emotions and how they work to affect the mind and body, and in my belief, to 'unhinge' them from innate equipoise.

And finally, Section III considers what within us, when

processed, may shift to hinge us back again to a sense of onward flow, which is stable and centred.

This book does not explore extreme forms of mental challenge, nor those that may have occurred at birth or through damage to the brain. Neither does it look at neurological diseases. It is a work that draws on research for films on anger, biotechnology and depression, as well as on professional and personal notes on patterns of the mind, over two decades. It infers from readings on India's centuries-old tradition of the mind. India has much to offer on wholeness and health.

I hope you find this of use, in unravelling deeper layers within, for your wellness or for that of loved ones and for the people you work with. Our inner-scape stealthily affects our relationships, both personal and professional.

Finally, mental and emotional wellness is a sense of fluidity, yet from a stable, central core. Such fluidity allows us to engage with change, without undue strain from an excess of any emotion. The power of emotions is immense, and if we understand them better, we may keep ourselves pleasantly and with awareness, in expansive balance.

SECTION I

NORMAL

We cannot change anything unless we accept it.

—Carl Gustav Jung,
Psychiatrist and psychoanalyst

ONE

THE SOCIAL NORMAL

The lady seated to my left on a flight mentioned that she and her husband lived in a family of 40 members. These were her husband's extended family—his parents, siblings, uncles, aunts and cousins. All of them lived together in a high-rise with several apartments, in the metropolis we were flying to. 'Forty?' I said, incredulously. 'Forty,' she said, calmly.

I grew up in a family of four—Mum, Dad, my brother and I. My father's work took him away from where his parents and younger siblings lived. Though he contributed to their well-being and participated in matters of importance, I think he was glad for his space, for a man who'd wanted to live and shape his own life. Contained and complete in our nuclear unit of four, visits to relatives were intermittent and unexciting for me, personally. My cousins were younger and I had little in common with them. Shy and socially awkward as a child, I was accustomed to my own devices and rhythm. If relatives came to stay, especially with a sense of entitlement as it often is, I'd feel an intrusion.

To then imagine 40 adults and children, continuously traversing through each other's lives and spheres, tore into my sense of order, quiet and privacy. What seemed normal to my co-passenger was quite the contrary to me—far from 'normal' and somewhat traumatic, even.

'Does it work?' I asked her, after several moments of silence.

'Well, if someone has a problem,' she said, 'especially in their business, then the men generally get together in a room. It happens often that one might know someone in a concerned department of the government. Another may know someone in banking or such sectors of assistance. They dig into each other's network and very quickly, there's a plan to take things ahead.'

'And is there a downside?' I asked.

She paused. 'Yes. There's no privacy...for the women...for the family.'

India is a land of communities. Caste, religion, profession, language and various other regional subcultures root the people of our country firmly within the identity of community. With 22 major languages, official sources additionally enlist 121 languages, several hundred dialects and subdialects, indicating known and identifiable communities to run into a few thousand.

Families from a particular caste, clan or community have often been led to live together, even until the second half of the twentieth century. This practice helped in the perpetuation of custom and tradition; it fostered a feeling of strength and security from numbers, and it allowed the community to access and share common resources. A village could house several different communities, where land and water are specifically allocated to each group.

On a trip to Rajasthan in 2013, our guide informed us that his village, Delwara, with close to 5,000 inhabitants, reflects such an arrangement. 'It has people from three different religious communities,' he said. 'Jains from the Shvetambar and Digambar sects, Shia and Sunni Muslims, and Hindus from 32 different sub-communities inhabit its space. On the basis of caste-profession, each wears a different style and colour of turban, each has access to a specified source of water and living space.'

With such an arrangement, order remains established only if all such diktats are followed without contention. Those who try to break these norms are commonly boycotted socially, and sometimes even threatened with violence.

A unit smaller than the community is the extended family, where two or more families live together, sharing common resources. The tradition may extend sometimes to four generations living on a common piece of land or under one roof. Originally, it may have sprung up around one man, as in the case of my co-passenger.

Her family's story may well have begun with a great grandfather or granduncle, similar to that of B. Chand. Chand had attended school till he was 15 and then left his village, in the 1940s, for better work opportunities. After a few odd jobs in the city, he landed himself at a jeweller's as an office boy and apprentice.

He began by delivering paper—invoices and designs—but gradually gained trust and grew in responsibility to deliver small pieces of jewellery to customers. Enterprising and alert, he learnt enough of the trade over the next nine years to found his own business of buying and selling semi-precious stones. His former employer was his first client, and through recommendation, his work expanded.

As did his family. He was married at 20 and had two children in quick succession. At the birth of his third child, a girl, he bought himself a small house, and christened it 'Laxmi Vilas, the abode of the goddess of wealth and fortune'. He named his daughter Laxmi, after the goddess, and regarded the little one as the bearer of good luck. Soon, he had his parents move in with him from the village. In time, other relatives came as well. His business, now of precious stones and gold, was growing rapidly and he needed people he could trust. Since his sons were still in school, he relied on a brother.

As work and family grew, so did the house. With another cousin and his family of five moving in, Chand bought himself a *kothi*, a house with more than one storey, and a modest bit of garden, both in front and at the rear. The women raised the children and took care of chores at home; the men attended to work and travelled to tap into suppliers and buyers across two states of India. By his mid-40s, the man bought himself a large bungalow with an adjoining estate.

Incontestable in his authority, his four grown-up sons eventually joined him in his business, and his three daughters were married off in their late teens. Each girl went to live with her husband and in-laws, as tradition demanded, to do their bidding.

Chand's brother, two cousins and their families lived with him and his kin. It was the normal, unquestionable thing to do since the business was of common interest, as was the estate as a living space. When laws changed, allowing apartments to be constructed, the bungalow was brought down to build what finally became an agglomeration of several apartments, allotting space to each individual family, as much as possible.

A small community thus arose from what is often called a 'joint family' (in this case, a rather large one) comprising more than one married couple and their children living together to pool and share resources. This was a 'normal' arrangement, a norm that spanned across clans and communities in several parts of India, until at least the late twentieth century.

For such an arrangement to continue, the line of command usually was, and still is, vested in the patriarch, the oldest male member within each family.[1] In villages, the community often selects a group of such patriarchs for collective decisions that centre around upholding and perpetuating the family and community structure, for men and even more so for women and youngsters, among other issues.

This social arrangement forms the backdrop to the story of two of the world's oldest sharpshooters, Chandro Tomar (88) and Prakashi Tomar (83). These women discovered their talent for shooting quite by chance, when they had accompanied Prakashi's daughter and Chandro's granddaughter to the local rifle shooting range, around 1998. Both women were in their 60s and grandmothers by then. Wedded to two brothers, they had lived together and supported each other through every stage of their married lives. To encourage their dithering young girls, they picked up the gun, aimed and shot. Each apparently hit bullseye.

The film, *Saand ki Aankh* or Bullseye[2] chronicles their journey to become national and international shooting champions. It portrays the challenges they faced as women to circumvent the rigid, patriarchal structure that does not permit women to think of things outside the purview of home. The film light-heartedly depicts the prevalent social arrangement—the women's chore-ridden lives packed with cooking, cleaning, working the fields, thawing the grain, tending to cattle, laying bricks and building houses, satisfying their husband's wants, desires and the need to produce a battalion of children (Chandro has eight and Prakashi has five), and tending to the demands of their growing families. All this in stark and ironic contrast to the husbands, who sit around smoking hookah between meals, deals and procreation, and shout orders and threats with a gun by their side to keep their authority undisputed. The women, children and grandchildren are terrified of approaching the elder men, from fear of upsetting them. The grandmother-shooters apparently spent more energy trying to get past the men, rather than on the contests. The competitions, in contrast, were a breeze.

About a fourth of Indian households perpetuate this system. Here, the social norm is to conform to an arrangement. 'Normal' is to accept what is unobtrusive to a given order. It is a pattern of expected, predictable conduct that doesn't stretch or challenge the status quo. Power of control thus remains unchallenged for the ones who wield it.

While families have broken down into smaller units, the

line of command remains largely unchanged. For most of us born in the 1970s and '80s, our grandparents, and at least one parent, if not both, had lived in a joint family set-up. Though education and exposure has led to allowances, early role models still influence the prevailing mindset. In an urban setting, too, irrespective of how large or small the unit is, the elder men or man assumes charge and priority. The arrangement plays itself out differently for the elderly, young adults and children of the family. Apparently, it can ease or stress, equally.

Primarily, whether rural or urban, this grouping provides comfort for the elderly. Where they have earned genuine respect, the system is often infused with warm regard and care. There is frequently someone at hand to attend to the ageing—sons and nephews along with their wives, daughters and grandchildren. Age signifies life experience and wisdom. Youngsters are tutored to approach seniors with respect. Young adults tend to their parents and other elder relatives with regard. They are sensitive to the elders' growing infirmity, often monitoring their needs and health emergencies, and also seeking their counsel. Elders, in turn, step in to babysit their grandchildren or fill in at home to support the work of their children. Each acts spontaneously out of his or her strength, without compulsion. Each can thus keep his or her dignity.

Even where family members move away, support is ensured—emotionally if not always physically. The fear that one may die alone—untended, disregarded and forgotten—is put to rest.

If, on the other hand, the bonds are not of love or genuine regard, this grouping becomes an imposition. Elders demand that sons and daughters-in-law attend to them, placing their needs and desires above the wishes of young adults at home. Young men and women may be expected to take permission for everything they do or plan—from a lunch out, to a holiday, to investments. They are often 'cut down to size' and 'kept in place' with what elders regard as correct and permissible. This degree of control is often dampening to the spirit of those whom it is thrust upon. The insecurity of losing control over others and over common resource can make the elderly indignant and, sometimes, militant in expression. In such cases, interference in the lives of younger adults becomes a right; expectation turns into entitlement.

For most families where parents live with married adult children (usually sons) and their families, the truth of the situation often oscillates between the pleasant and the unpleasant. To keep a certain balance within the system, power and obligations are often negotiated on a daily basis, between different members. *Do my bidding, and I will sanction your request*, is typically the underlying, unspoken understanding. Those who are familiar with these dynamics can use the system to their advantage, but for those who are uncomfortable or unaccustomed to it, it can prove exhausting.

While the demand for acquiescence is strong, it isn't uncommon for an elder to reach out with trust and love. A friend of mine, for instance, found herself estranged from her husband, for a few years. The loving, unconditional presence of her mother-in-law, however, helped her stay in the marriage. The elder took over the reins of the home, monitoring the kitchen, the household and the demands of the grandchildren, and encouraged her daughter-in-law to concentrate on work instead. By the time the older lady passed away, the marriage had regained stability. 'Even if I had walked out of the marriage, she would have supported me. My mother-in-law was that kind of person. She could see the truth,' the younger woman says, in remembrance.

Another acquaintance and his wife decided to end their marriage of 20 years. While the husband moved out to find a place of his own, the lady, along with their children, chose to live with her ageing father-in-law. Over the years, she had grown to trust the older man's counsel. He had always treated her as a daughter and, she, in turn, looked up to him as her own father.

For children, with more adults in a family unit, the dynamics work in varied ways.

My co-passenger in the flight, mentioned earlier, told me that her 10-year-old son always had company. Three of his cousins, in fact, were in his class. 'If one of them is ill, catching up is never a problem!' she said.

'They get along well, do they?' I asked.

'Well, mostly,' she said. 'One of them, he really hates!' she said with a laugh. 'But he loves two of his cousin sisters more than his own brother, I think. They are always together and encouraging each other.'

The boy's tenderness towards his cousin sisters had, in turn, strengthened the bond between the two mums. They were sisters-in-law, around the same age, married to two brothers. They'd become friends, and had grown to support and care for each other's needs. 'I can travel alone to visit my mother, because I know that my sister-in-law will take care of my sons, as she does her two daughters,' my co-passenger said.

The boy, in effect, has more than one caregiver, a common phenomenon within this order of family. It works as a check, especially if the child is not inclined to listen to a parent.

I've seen it at work. One afternoon, at a family lunch, my husband's niece, then 9 years old, left the table with her plate half full of food. 'Finish your chicken,' her mother said to her. Four of us adults instinctively glanced at her plate. 'I've finished,' the child said, brushing aside her mother's request. We all gently chided her, almost in unison. The force of so many voices led her back to the table. She sat and finished her lunch.

Since 2005, child psychologists have undertaken intermittent studies to understand if the structure of joint families is more conducive to the health, ability and well-being of a child. Since there are several more adults or caregivers in the same space, such research tried to study whether children from joint families scored higher on tests of physical and psychological health. Also, with cousins growing up together, would they be more adaptive socially than children from nuclear families that comprise one married couple and their children?

In one study,[3] over 200 participants were chosen from a mid-sized town in northern India. The subjects were in their early teens. The group was levelled out in terms of socio-economic status and other variables. The final sample was almost equally from both joint as well as nuclear families. They all had stay-at-home mothers and demonstrated a healthy and strong relationship with their caregivers.

The findings were interesting. On mental ability, particularly intelligence and reasoning, children from nuclear families scored marginally higher than those from joint families. On physical health, once again children from nuclear families scored better. This was surprising, since the assumption is that children in larger families are attended to better, with more adults around. Lastly, on wellness, which included a sense of security and positivity, the difference was marginal, with the scores tipping in favour of nuclear families.

The researchers concluded that it wasn't so much the numbers as much as the nature of bonding that matters. A child needs a stable and loving presence in his/her caregiver for a strong bond to form, rather than the presence of several adults. It can sometimes be confusing for a child to receive excessive instruction from too many people, especially if there's conflict in opinion or palpable disharmony between adults. What matters more is the quality of attachment to one person, and its stability, rather than numbers.

It was also observed that children in nuclear families were more independent than children from joint families. This was probably because they were entrusted with more responsibility of looking after themselves. Guided by the trust between child and parent, the former took greater initiative in their own welfare. There was less or no opportunity at home for 'group thinking', when several children follow the lead of one or two others, often mindlessly, thus pulling and averaging the level of general intelligence of the group to a lower measure than its individual components.

A specific study on social behaviour found children from joint families to lead.[4] The presence of parents, uncles, aunts, grandparents and cousins of various ages offer these children an array of role models. Familiarity with relatives from different age groups, experts concluded, had made the children more adaptive in their interactions within the family, in comparison with children from single unit families. They were more willing to share and empathize with cousins or uncles and aunts they felt a close bond with.

But with two variables, the results changed. The first was technology. Children who spent more time absorbed in screens—mobile phones, computers or TV—were less well behaved than those who spent less than a couple of hours a day absorbed in gadgets. It didn't matter whether the family was a joint or a nuclear one. The second and more crucial determinant was the environment at home. Where that was positive and secure, children displayed better behaviour, irrespective of joint or nuclear status.

On the point of better social skills, Dr Deepali Rao[5], a clinical psychologist practising in Delhi, holds a counterview. 'Children from joint families have more opportunity to interact,' she says, 'but on the other hand, they tend to restrict their interactions to the family. They may not actively seek and learn from interactions with peers outside the family. As a result, social experience and learning may be limited.'

'On the other hand, children from nuclear families may actually compensate well for fewer family members and turn to peers for social interaction. Their approach is a more open-minded one. Those from joint families may not necessarily develop skills of tolerance and empathy outside the immediate family,' says Dr Rao. This may, therefore, strengthen bonds among family members, but may pitch them more aggressively towards outsiders. It can feed into the 'us versus them' syndrome.

Thus, the effect of large family units on children seems to span a gamut. Comfort in numbers may make children boisterous, but in terms of confidence, intelligence, sensitivity and responsibility, the stability and a sense of nurturing a child may receive and share with his/her caregiver, matters more than the structure and size of the family he/she belongs to.

With many members of a family living together, the definition of 'normal' spills over into other aspects as well. Consider what might be 'normal expression'. Close relatives living together rub off on each other and often sound alike, even if they may not look alike. I knew a family of seven siblings who, for no reason or defect, all spoke with an unusual softening of 't'. One could tell they were of a flock!

Sound, manner and styles of expression are passed down and around. If loud and rough is what goes around, then children usually pick up the same language and tone. With strength in numbers, things spoken or done get reinforced several times over.

Similarly, values and beliefs are transmitted, whatever they are.

This is why communities prefer young people marrying within the same community—for the transition to be as seamless as possible. It would be easier, presumably, for a young woman to adapt to a similar home, with similar customs and traditions. For the family receiving the young bride, their expectations wouldn't be out of sync, either.

These expectations usually abide by defined roles and responsibilities, especially where patriarchy is embedded. Even as the numbers of joint family units fall, and those of nuclear families rise, the extended family exists as well—relatives having nuclear family units, who still remain connected to the larger family commune through shared property, business interests or common beliefs. Where members deviate from the structure, the larger family or community enforces, subtly or blatantly, what it regards as normal and correct—that the men attend to the affairs of business and property and the women manage the home, collectively if the family is large. No resistance is expected to this arrangement. Further, the women must iron out any differences they may have among themselves. In educated families, an unmarried daughter may join the family business or be encouraged to do her own thing. However, once married, the prerogative of her continuing her work usually lies with what is acceptable to her husband and in-laws.

Even if women work, home is primarily their responsibility. It cuts across social and economic class or strata. Women are expected to manage domestic affairs, and make the children compliant, with emphasis on the girls, who are required to be responsible and obedient to impositions on them. The boys are usually allowed a greater degree of independence and indulgence. The effect is a disproportionate sense of entitlement.

I recall an instance at an after-screening event, in a small town. The little gathering that stayed on spontaneously broke into song. It so happened that all the women sung in tune, while two young men who insisted on singing had no sense of melody whatsoever. They sang loudly, confident of the lyrics flashing on their mobile screens, ruining song after song. Finally, a couple of ladies requested them to rest their voices for a bit. 'But we know all the lyrics,' one of them objected, as a counter. 'Let the ladies sing this one song,' one young woman asserted. The boys were totally perplexed. One of them glared at her. The other seemed dampened, not knowing how to react. Evidently, they were unaccustomed to being told to back off or, as in this case, to shut up. To be inhibited, in any way, is not usually part of the male narrative. Since they were grossly outnumbered, they complied, though unhappily.

Strength in numbers feeds into reinforcing family structure and gender roles as advantageous for one group in other aspects. A study[6] conducted in a large town of central India revealed that two-thirds of the men from joint families felt 'moderately loaded' with work, and only 20 per cent felt they were 'heavily loaded', because they could share the burden of the common business with other male family members. Sixty-eight per cent of men from nuclear families, on the other hand, felt they were 'heavily loaded' with work and responsibility, as the onus wasn't shared.

For the women, the scale flipped. Fifty per cent women in nuclear families felt loaded with work and responsibility, while 68 per cent of women from joint families felt their workload was excessive. The reason for this is that when there are more members in the family, housework increases manifold. It can be rigorous and ceaseless. Men generally regard domestic chores a woman's domain, and do not offer to help. It doesn't serve their image. This is true for male children as well, who are often fed with a sense of entitlement over their sisters, and absolved of all household chores. This instruction leaves them ill-equipped and inept to look after their own needs, and so they demand priority and charge as the only way to get by. The system leans to perpetuate itself.

Sometimes, force is used to keep people and structure in place. Violence is not uncommon, irrespective of economic or social standing. The more entrenched the family or community is in attitudes of male domination, the greater the chances for violence as a way to subdue a non-compliant woman or child. The study quoted above revealed that domestic violence against women was 90 per cent higher in the joint families of the sample group of 50 joint families than in the 50 nuclear units. This is surprising, since one would assume that women are more alone and vulnerable in a nuclear family, while in joint families, the presence of elders and others would provide ample opportunity for intervention. However, if domestic violence is already a norm within a certain family set-up, then the perpetrator would use this as an acceptable method to make a woman submissive, and to warn others as well. Many men, together endorsing a particular view, would embolden the approach. So, while the women may comfort each other after a battering, taking on the structure may prove too daunting in such cases.

'Normal', within the larger Indian community, is often taken to narrowly mean compliance, for better or worse, and to merge your *self* into things that keep the established arrangement in place. A family commune doesn't just pool resources. Individual *identities* too are poured within a collective pool. Appearance, expression, thought and identity, all are led to smelt into the larger mould.

Those who are naturally compliant or are conditioned to be so, may have little cause for grief. They can draw on the support such a set-up offers, and take comfort and strength in numbers. Those who wish to pursue their own path, men or women, more often than not, come up against the inflexibility of the structure. A person with thoughts, aspiration and plans of his/her own poses a threat to the *raison d'etre*, routine and resource arrangement of the family or community. If a man or woman is allowed his/her bidding, others might want it too. That would endanger the system and its comfort zone; it might even take it apart, especially if property or business has to be split into individual shares. Where violence isn't an option, the pressure of ostracism is. Men and women who display differences are often ridiculed. If they defy the line of authority or order, they are actively disrespected, ignored and sometimes, disinherited.

This is not to say that community does not offer a sense of belonging. People thrive on their sense of community, and on bonds, both strong and casual. In 1973, Mark Granovetter, a sociologist at Stanford University, offered a paper titled 'The Strength of Weak Ties', which discussed how 'weak ties' or light-hearted exchange with acquaintances led to a person feeling happy and connected. Granovetter suggested that while the quality of our relationships matter, quantity of connections matters as well.

Within large families too, people thrive on their varied interactions. It keeps members engaged and busy, and gives them a sense of purpose and meaning when they are able to participate in the lives of others. A positive sense of community often extends beyond family. I recall reading about an incident a few years ago, when a man's car broke down, in the southern part of the US. His phone was out of charge and he said he tried to flag help for hours. Finally, a Mexican couple and their children stopped to help him fix his car. Then, they drove off a hundred yards, but returned to offer him their food, since 'he must be hungry so long on the road'. Touched, the man sat on the road and cried, he wrote. I remember thinking such hospitality is not unusual where community bonds are strong.

Closer home, a friend's son is a musician in another city. On one occasion, he turned up somewhat ill to tutor a young girl, but the student's grandmother did not allow him to take the class. Instead, she sat him down for a sandwich and coffee. She then gave him fruit for the rest of the day, so he would not be careless about eating. My friend, a thousand miles away, was ever so grateful to this elder stranger for looking after her son.

In another instance, a friend living in a remote place in the hills of northern India lost her husband. Within an hour, some 30 men from the nearby village reached her place, and took over the arrangements of all that needed to be done. 'All I did was make one call to the priest,' she said. 'They did everything else. Four women came to help my cook make tea and refreshments for everyone present. They hung around until the cremation. After the cremation, they gave me the death certificate. I didn't even know who went and had it done.'

Community thus reaches out in many ways. It holds the power to support or obstruct. What matters is whether its offering of support is genuine, or whether its demands in return are intrusive and interfering in tone. 'Weak ties', in their very nature, allow us to be pleasant. These are exchanges that do not permit interference into our lives. Feeling connected with a chorus group at a weekly practice, or 'friends' on social media may foster a sense of community, but are still mild interactions that are made out of choice. They do not feature the heavy-handed compliance that a community or family may feel entitled to demand from its members.

Such heavy-handedness leads to an unwieldy 'social normal', as discussed earlier, and can cause significant and continuous stress and strain to play out as serious disorders. Enforced compliance within the family and community itself has at its root the fear of losing control and power over resource and people, and the fear of being defied. Indignation is usually the first sign of this fear, not only from the men, but also from the women, who've spent a lifetime complying with the rigidity of the system. They give up their personal aspirations, often sandwiched between the needs and demands of their in-laws and children, to expect some authority and security in old age. Permitting the young ones to do their own thing now would mean breaking the cycle, to sign away the promise of dominion and security that comes with being a certain age. Roles defined are thus fiercely guarded and imposed.

Where allowances are made in recognizing differences, it is often as an indulgence. The daughter-in-law may or may not be so readily encouraged for her abilities, but doting grandparents proudly speak of how 'different and talented' their gadget-savvy grandchildren (girls or boys) are. Indeed, a deluge in opportunities and exposure for children who are plugged into the internet has challenged traditional trajectories and opened up alternative paths for career and expression. An acquaintance's son is an aeronautics engineer in the making. He's been modelling airplanes since he was six. Another friend's teen daughter has had a book of poems published, and yet another's nine-year-old son is a serious self-taught chef. Stories of children determining their futures abound, sometimes within homes of urban, educated professionals, who have gone against a given order wherever necessary to support and promote their children's passions. They are aware and sensitive as parents and might make 'fun' in-laws as well. The men are often equitable in approach. Some are hands-on at home, and many of the women are career professionals or stay-at-home moms or wives, out of choice. It is a shift ahead from the dominant parochial mindset.

But even as children and youngsters have more options in self-expression than earlier, whether the expectations from a boy and more so from a girl's future life—in terms of marriage, children and/or family—have changed in any significant way, remains to be seen.

Further, there is no conclusive data on how much social

influence this professional class may wield to dent millennia of the patriarchal norm, which still reigns unchallenged across large swaths of the country, in both rural and urban areas—at home, at work and in spaces between each. Women professionals come up against it numerous times a day—from the surly taxi driver who silently disapproves of their independence, to the peon or subordinate who is disdainful about taking orders from a woman, to a colleague in a multinational firm who can't have a woman's work or suggestion be better than his, to elders who regard an informed and confident woman as too 'forward' for their comfort. The list goes on. Much of India's workforce, in urban metropolises as well, comprises of migrant workers from villages in far-flung states. They make up the band of security guards, delivery boys, construction workers, vendors, drivers, office or home support staff and often fresh recruits within the ranks of the cops as well. With exceptions, many in this workforce have little or no concept of an urban woman and, in their own way, work to reinforce patriarchal dominance. They believe that a woman's place is at home. Any variance from the norm, leaves her open to threat, from slight to serious.

The man who doesn't fit the alpha-male image faces similar pressures. Bullying or name-calling is common to those who appear 'different'. It is a spill over from the fact that anything challenging the established 'norm', in any way, is open to ridicule, threat and even violence. In an extreme incident a few years ago, shopkeepers from South Delhi taunted a young man from the Northeast for his shock of coloured hair. When he objected and retaliated, seven men beat him up with sticks. Though the fight was broken up and he went home, he didn't wake up the next day. His injuries proved fatal.[7]

Such intimidation bears out significantly on one's mental and emotional health. To incessantly negotiate obstruction and threat at every step, both outside as well as within the home, sparks aggression and upheaval within. The inner mechanism, the self, is thrown into disarray.

For women, the effect is exponential. A woman is the loci of each family unit and her peace and happiness, from being appreciated for who she is, touches all in the family. If inhibited, disregarded and shaken in her emotional fabric, within or outside the home, the children would soak in her vulnerability to be affected the most, after her.

The social normal, as the ecosphere within which one negotiates life on a daily basis, may thus contain within its rigidity of structures and tone, the seed of emotional tumult. The force of what it deems 'normal' can prod emotional circuits that may compel an intense unsettling, within.

A strong community could act as an agent to either encourage or extinguish individual potential. Family size, joint or nuclear, could work either way as well. Background experience and expectation, as we shall see, are factors in play. 'Normal', as a relative phenomenon, hinges on who outlines it, and for whom.

TWO

THE GENDER NORMAL

I came across a young woman in Delhi, who was from a nuclear family of modest means. She was the older of two sisters. In 2005, she married a man from a well-to-do, though conservative, family. They'd met at a common friend's place and were drawn to each other. They courted for a year before settling down.

The boy's parents, however, were unhappy with the fact that their son was seeing someone below their social strata. Yet, after some discussion, they agreed to the marriage, since the girl was fair-skinned! It assured the family a greater chance for their progeny to have lighter skin (a colonial hangover). However, the family of the young man laid out a condition. The girl wouldn't be allowed to work after marriage. The boy supported his parents' decision.

This isn't an infrequent condition or practice. It ostensibly stems from a wish to protect young women, from the vagaries and threats of the outside world, if they so desire and if the family has the means to do so. 'The women in my house needn't go out to work, because I can provide for them,' is the underlying sentiment. On the other hand, where it isn't presented as a choice, it arises from and feeds off chauvinism, where set roles unquestioningly place the woman within the house, irrespective of her abilities and interests. Mobility and/or financial freedom of the woman are often opposed since they may empower her to be her own person. She would have the means to do as she chooses, at variance with what elders at home or her husband might desire. Keeping her at home allows greater control over her life, and maintains the status quo of women being relegated to domestic chores and responsibilities.

A few months after the wedding, the young woman found herself bored and listless. Noticing this, her father-in-law offered to pay her a modest amount for every dish she cooked that met his approval. The girl's interests lay elsewhere. Though she knew how to cook, it wasn't the thing to spur her on. Before marriage, she had worked in retail as an assistant to a designer for a chain of stores. Her job had brought her in contact with clients from all over, as well as with employees from different departments. She thrived on those random interactions and in her sense of creative independence.

Her father-in-law's 'incentive' proved inadequate. As she felt increasingly constrained, her spirits sunk lower and she became irritable with time. So the family conferred that having a child would take her mind away from the things she might have wanted to pursue. It would keep her busy and things would settle. As is often the case across social and economic standing, progeny is the prominent reason for marriage—a child, especially a son, to carry forth the family 'name'.

Confused and under pressure, the woman conceived. Her pregnancy was difficult and it made her feel increasingly disorientated. All around though, she saw happy and eager faces. That brought her fleeting moments of comfort, but mostly, it fuelled her sense of rage at their apathy towards the tumult she was experiencing within. She felt her world was coming apart. She was hurtling towards an event that she was unprepared for. There was new life growing within her body, and she wasn't completely in accord with this decision. Her physical discomfort—nausea, fatigue and lack of sleep—heightened her helplessness and agitation.

She gave birth to a baby girl, who was slightly underweight but otherwise physiologically sound. The baby's father was delighted; his parents, not so much. They'd hoped for a boy. Their sense of resignation was the tipping point. The young woman slipped into depression. 'Postpartum depression,' her doctor explained. 'It's normal.' The young mother felt a crushing pointlessness, as if she'd signed her life away.

Unable to get back to her chores, her depression was whispered about when relatives came visiting. 'They gave you a defective piece,' she overheard a relative comment, on her and her parents. It enraged her, but she bottled it up within, physically and mentally exhausted with the events that had taken over her life. Every day, she felt she was falling further behind. She attended to the child in a daze, thinking it to be a bad dream from which she might awaken.

Her husband tended to her as much as he could. In the few moments that she responded, he felt reassured. He tried to comfort her, but after a point, would get impatient, when 'she wouldn't pull herself together'. He too believed their roles were set and there was only this much he could do. Didn't she know that? 'She has everything,' he would say in exasperation, with reference to material comfort, 'what else does she want?'

When he despaired, he'd turn to his mother. Not an unkindly soul, she would reassure him. 'She'll be fine. It takes a while to come around,' she'd say. It had taken her the first 12 years of marriage to find peace with *he*r mother-in-law, in the house they'd shared until the latter's death, a few years earlier. Her wishes had been subservient to those of her in-laws; the same was expected of her daughter-in-law. Nothing was out of the expected, out of the ordinary, or not normal.

The need for independent expression can prove paramount for emotional equilibrium. This young lady felt stripped of her choice to professionally engage with people and the world, as she might have liked to. Her happiness and a sense of self hinged on her being proactive, rather than being a mute participant in things thrust upon her. Within her framework, she craved her privacy, both mentally and physically. Yet, the same parameters she desired, could prove unsettling for another. Consider the next example.

Neeti grew up in a large, animated setting, with her parents, her dad's two brothers and their families, and much hustle and bustle around her. Of her six cousins, she was particularly close to two sisters. They did everything together, as much as possible. When she was 23, her uncle's friend suggested a suitable match. The boy was an information technology professional with his own start-up. He was pleasant and well-travelled. He lived with his parents and his older sister, who was single.

When they met for the first time, Neeti instantly liked him. A few months later, they were married. She moved in to live with his family. Though it was still a joint family, with many adults at home, the unit was much smaller and quieter than what she was accustomed to. 'After a meal, everyone would go to their own room,' she said. 'It was depressing!'

In time, though, Neeti was able to find an equilibrium. There were no restrictions or diktats that she was expected to follow, besides a basic courtesy and regard for her in-laws. Her husband doted on her. When his mother tried to play the proverbial mother-in-law soon after their marriage, he told her to take it easy. His father supported him in this decision, and told his wife to leave the girl alone.

Importantly, Neeti met with her family regularly. She and her cousins continued to go out together. Unlike a more conservative family set-up that bars a married woman from visiting her maternal home often or without consent 'so that she may adjust in her new home', there were no such restrictions in this educated, open-minded family. It was up to her how she chose to employ her time. Met with less force, less resistance to her keeping her happiness, Neeti was able to pull herself through the initial low.

In a third instance, a young woman from a conservative community in western India married a young man from the same community. The marriage was arranged, as it often is in such communities. His was an unprogressive family. No one could cross his father for fear of the man's temper. His mother had learnt to deal with it, but he and his brother were terrified of their father. His bride, cultured and educated, was taken aback at the tone of every interaction in her husband's family, with whom she spent a few weeks after the wedding. However, soon after, she travelled to the UK to be with her husband.

Two of his friends at work helped her settle down. She was from a bustling joint family, with uncles, aunts, cousins and grandparents living together. Here, she found herself alone and estranged. Unable to work, she took to pursuing a course that would qualify her for a job later.

In the interim, however, she and her husband began having trouble in their relationship. He wanted a child; she wanted time. Unsettled and alone, and too far away from home, the girl became miserable. She held herself back from divulging her state of mind when her family called. She didn't want them to worry. Her father had lost a substantial amount in an investment gone wrong. That too deterred her from pulling them into what she considered her own negativity. She fought her feelings, chiding herself to look instead at the bright side of things, but the gap between the love and company of her own family and her new life was much to bear. She felt herself losing interest and energy.

Things were exacerbated when her in-laws came to stay for several weeks. Though she'd wake up early, get dressed in their traditional attire (as was expected) and kept breakfast ready by the time they surfaced, she found no appreciation. Intelligent and informed, she would often refute what her father-in-law said. He didn't like that. Unaccustomed to being challenged even in conversation, several altercations followed, each with a verbal violence she was unaccustomed to. Her husband tried to make peace, but she was the outsider at the end. Her request to have him curtail his father's abusive language went unaddressed. He couldn't bring himself to stand up to his father. As a child, he'd hid in the washroom when his father's temper turned dark and agressive. His mother had learnt to stay silent. By the time they left, the young woman felt bewildered, shaken and deeply dejected by her predicament.

Normal is thus a relative concept. It is contextual—where you come from and where you find yourself. In all three cases, the women felt uprooted. The environment they had grown up in was different from the one they found themselves in after marriage. This new 'normal' they were expected to conform to wasn't wide enough to take their mental and emotional well-being into account. While Neeti was able to adapt, with support and warmth from her new family, the other two young women found themselves estranged and compromised in a way that shook their sense of wellness.

In a social context, the norm is an expected pattern of behaviour. 'Normal', from the Latin *norma*, indeed translates as 'pattern' or 'rule'. For many, it comes to mean what is mostly seen or what we see the most of.

In India, for most parts of it, the norm is for the woman to move out of her parental home, and usually settle in with the family of the husband. In the third case too, had the young man not been working abroad, his wife would have had little or no option but to live with her in-laws. Resistance to do so would be, and often is, regarded as an affront. Patterns are thus perpetuated.

Since the norm is an established one, the boys are usually brought up to believe the same—that they won't be the ones necessarily uprooted, after marriage. All arrangements remain the same, as it has always been, but for the addition of the new bride. For that, some adjustments may be made. The onus to settle in, though, remains on the young woman. This is her new family and she needs to find her groove within it. If she opposes it, then she isn't necessarily a 'good' person. If she resists it forcefully, then there's something abnormal about her.

The pressures that a rigid, social structure exerts on the women, also constrains the men, who are equally conditioned, though with a difference in emphasis. For the man, the normal thing to do is to be the provider. That automatically ensures his authority at home. For his life to be within the purview of 'normal', he needs to have a family—a wife who would tend to his needs and those of his parents, and bear him children. His duty is also towards his parents and the elders in the extended family. He is expected to look after them and to surrender his wishes and those of his family to theirs.

To fulfil these responsibilities and obligations, he needs to have work that ensures him a regular income. His latent talents or propensities, if different from such leanings, may not find active support or encouragement.

His success is measured through his material wealth and through the compliance of his wife and children to his word and wishes, and then as he assumes the role of the patriarch, the submission of his children's spouses and his grandchildren to his domination. The more successful the man is perceived to be, the more his authority should reflect in the affairs at home. Since he is the one in touch with the outside world, through work and travel, his wisdom and counsel are considered absolute. Any contrarian view is regarded a breach in image. This arrangement varies in degree between man and wife, based on how their relationship builds over the years, yet this is usually the overarching framework, the starting premise, from which boundaries may then be somewhat pushed.

For the men who wish to know life differently, the pressures are enormous. First, they need to battle a rigid mental construct, this set path laid out in front of them, reinforced solidly and subtly, through the structure of family and community. Men who'd rather explore their creative abilities, than their leanings towards engineering, medicine, family business or IT, for instance, were for a long time considered lost to the real world. A well-known author, before he gained repute, lived in his parents' outhouse for several years when he was well past his 30s. Though supported by family and recognized for his brilliance, friends and associates nonetheless considered him a drop-out, a failure in the real world, until one of his books became a bestseller. Once his name was known, all was accepted as part of an inevitable trajectory. Others may not be so fortunate. A man who doesn't 'make it' can be easily disregarded and dismissed, irrespective of his talents, sensitivity or thoughts.

Men who wish to branch out of the family fold to independently carve out a role in life for themselves encounter reluctance from their elders, who would rather the youngsters adhere to the professional plans approved by their fathers. Their personal lives should meet the approval of their mothers. Anything less may often be considered disloyal, even a betrayal.

But for most men so conditioned, this definition of 'normal' seems reasonable and suitable. It assures them an advantage over women and children, and over younger siblings. They consider it one less thing to deal with. If a man thinks otherwise, the first opposition, to what is perceived as his 'losing control' over wife and children, comes from peers and elders. They feel the structure will be threatened, were he allowed to do so. It takes an exceptionally secure man to break out of this image.

For those who cling unthinkingly to this framework, the adverse effects on personal growth and subsequently on mental health are inescapable. A man, undisputed in authority or at least expecting to be so, can grow his ego and the image of his self-worth to alarming proportions. The more he grows in self-importance, the less he listens to the voices—concerns, considerations and wishes—of others around him. He may believe he is in control of things, situations and people, but in actuality, his need to be in control can enslave him and drive him to internal unrest. It can make him unduly demanding, touchy and reactionary. He begins to assume that the happiness of others is also under his command. Only what he allows, must go—every opportunity for fun and joy should also meet his approval and seek his consent.

This is a vicious cycle. His assumed right to know every going-on can make him unnecessarily suspicious. In extreme cases, he can get violent—verbally and physically, since he becomes less equipped to handle critique or opposition in any measure. Rather than evolve and flow, his internal fabric is taut and stressed. The wisdom of age and experience can be lost on him, if instead of becoming expansive, inclusive and considerate with it, he contracts in his vision to focus on the 'I, me and myself'. Unprepared to let go pleasantly, he instead is hounded by the prospects of the loss of social relevance. His need for constant attention can make him seem obnoxious and unbearable to the people around him.

Apart from the consequences of this inflexible stance on his own mental and emotional well-being, his immediate family members or his work associates may be subjected to mental anguish. In one case, on a social visit to a well-known entrepreneur's place for tea, an elderly manager from his office came to deliver a file. The entrepreneur glanced at it, and short of flinging it back at the manager, lost no time in shouting him down for a minor inadequacy he'd spotted. He belittled the manager in front of the guests and worse, in the presence of his eight-year-old granddaughter. The manager, flushed with humiliation, left the room without a word. If this was routine for both employer and employee, it was unpleasant for us, but more so for the little child, who promptly left the room in shocked protest.

In another case, DP, a civil contractor, lived with his wife, their elder son and his mother. A younger son was working in another city.

When his elder son got married, the daughter-in-law, as the norm demands, came to live with the family. Within a month of the wedding, DP began spending more time at home. He wanted his daughter-in-law's attention. He expected her to be around him and take care of him through the day. The young bride was taken aback. What seemed like affection felt like an intrusion into the little privacy she'd hoped to have. Her husband and mother-in-law explained to her that DP had sometime in the past expressed the desire for a daughter. To fill that void, he was probably showering his attention on her, or rather craving for hers.

Despite this explanation, the young woman could not handle her father-in-law's aggression. Whenever she failed to pander to his constant need for attention, DP would get verbally abusive towards the entire family. If his wife or son requested him to take it easy, he'd shout even louder, so that his daughter-in-law and neighbours were able to hear his displeasure. The unpleasantness at home increased, and the young bride became terrified and stressed. When her husband would come home after work, she would often break down.

After several months, without any signs of the situation letting up, her husband advised her to take a break and arranged for her to travel to her parents' home. A couple of weeks later, when she returned, the father-in-law created a scene. He said that she should have sought his permission to go home in the first place.

Around this time, the younger son came visiting. He'd been away from home for two years and found it hard to adjust to his father's need to dominate. One day, he cut short his visit and without informing anyone stayed away at a friend's for a few days. This loss of control further upset and distressed his father.

The daughter-in-law, unable to deal with the worsening situation at home, once again left for her parents' home. This time, DP asked his son to call up her parents and tell them that if she didn't return immediately, divorce papers would be filed against her. The son, under pressure to deal with an unreasonable demand, somehow managed to request his wife to come back.

When she did, DP confronted her, accusing her and her parents of demeaning and humiliating him. The next day, the young girl and her husband left home, without informing DP or his wife, and checked into a hotel. When he realized they'd left, DP had a bout of restlessness and complained of uneasiness. He told his wife to admit him to the nearby hospital, and to inform his elder son and daughter-in-law.

In this case, DP and his family were considered normal people. Neighbours and relatives thought nothing of the fact that DP expected to rule over his flock and have his daughter-in-law attend to him. Here, nothing was construed as amiss. The trauma this generated for his sons and daughter-in-law, and for his wife, though, was immense. It kept them on tenterhooks at the very least, and deeply impacted the young couple's sense of wellness and hope for the future. Through the next few years, they had to re-negotiate their lives and resources, which put the young man under strain. He would vent his frustration on his wife. Though things have somewhat settled since, the stress of the first few years of marriage still plays itself out in their relationship.

One man's 'normal' sense of entitlement can severely tear into the peace of others.

THREE

THE SEXUAL-SENSUAL NORMAL

SEXUALITY

The sexual urge, a natural, potent one, can be raw and violent. Over millennia, the larger body of traditional Indian literature has stressed ways and methods to refine this urge. It propounds that the nature of lust, in its force, is driven by the primary urge to satisfy itself. Under the powerful influence of such force, an individual may be led to disregard and hurt the other.

Much of our traditional tenets, therefore, abound in ways to transform the raw power of this energy (and of any other for that matter), into vigour that is aesthetic and empowering for one and all. Such thought advises sensitivity and sometimes, restraint. As an individual choice, for those in quest of things profound, it offers ways for the rawness of this energy to transmute, entirely.

What seems to largely manifest in society, however, is repression and suppression. Talking about sex in India is often taboo. Rarely will a mother speak about it to her son or her daughter. In the 1990s, sex education in school was limited to knowing about the menstrual cycle. Girls would be segregated and then shown a presentation. The few boys who would slink into the viewing space would snigger or stare suggestively at the girls. Education on sex has been included into the curriculum since then, but teachers, uncomfortable to talk about it, often skip it, and sometimes refuse to teach it.

Even now, men, through large parts of the country, are brought up to feel a sense of entitlement in their desire to satiate their sexual urge. In such circuits, consent or an equitable approach towards a woman and her desire is considered a weakness. While the contrary does exist, approaching a woman with regard for her, championed by sensitive and secure men, it is yet not enough to prevail as the dominant disposition.

Women, on the other hand, are dissuaded from discussing sex or exploring their needs. Women often teach women to be submissive, to 'find a good husband and household'. Submissive is 'decent', and men expect the same as well.

MT and his wife BT sought to see a counsellor. Their marriage was a traditional, arranged one. It had been a year. She accused him of not being able to satisfy her sexually; he was shocked and angered at the fact that this was a consideration for her. He would trip on his words just trying to approach the topic.

With heterosexual relationships so rigidly defined, there is little scope for any other form of sexual expression. The effect of this on inner processes can be profound.

PK and his four siblings had a privileged upbringing during a time when the country was struggling with limited opportunities.

At university, PK befriended a group of three young men, one of whom he was particularly attentive to. In school, he had always kept the company of boys. It was normal for 'good boys' from his community to strictly stay away from the girls. Occasionally, he would acknowledge the friends of his sisters. The fact that he seemed uninterested in pursuing girls was pleasantly construed as decent and appropriate behaviour by his parents.

In college, he sparked to life. Confident and animated, he seemed to come into his own. His parents noted this change in him, pleasantly. Then, much to the consternation of his mother, his grades began to fall. She realized he was spending all his time with his three friends, one in particular. She blamed his father for spoiling their only son by giving him a motorcycle and enough money to 'gallivant all day long'. It bothered her that he seemed defiant to everything she suggested and was bent on doing his bidding.

By the time he graduated, PK had fallen out with his friends. He no longer talked or hung out with his 'best friend'. Even a random mention of the other boy's name by his sisters in passing would make PK silent and surly.

The dynamics at home, however, had changed for him. He felt estranged from his family. His father attributed this as a passing phase. His mother felt that her son had lost track in these three years. He seemed distracted and unwilling to commit himself to work. Irritable and unresponsive to her affections, PK had grown indifferent to his sisters.

After whiling a year away, PK joined an uncle's business of tea exports. The moment he seemed to settle into his work, his parents arranged for him to meet a suitable girl. He was in his early 20s, and marriage was the appropriate and obvious episode to follow. The girl they selected seemed affable to him. He went along with their wishes, excited to enter a new phase of life.

Over the next eight years, PK settled into work and family. Part of it was exigency. His father had met with a fatal accident, and as the only son, he had to take on the mantle of heading the family. He had three children. When their son was born, he felt that they could stop having more kids. His family was now 'complete'. Work was engaging and secure. They had no pressing worries financially. It all seemed good and normal. Yet, he often complained of being under stress and seemed restless and irritable.

An unfamiliar contempt built up in him, which he directed at the women. Though still tender with his little daughters, he was derisive of his wife's wishes, and palpably angry at his mother. 'I will do what I want!' was his retort each time one of the women approached him with a request or a suggestion. When his sisters called, he was brusque. 'This is not right!' his mother would say. 'I don't care what you think is right!' he would snap back, cutting short any further discussion. It seemed the 'right' things were driving him asunder; he began to indulge in the forbidden ones.

He started by drinking. Fond of his drink on social occasions, he began to fix three stiff ones every evening at home. His wife was appalled. His mother, who lived with them, was more vocal about it, and forbade him from drinking at home. He responded by doubling his intake. Within a year, he was addicted.

He'd hit the bottle early evening, as soon as he'd be back from work. A sense of dread would creep into the household. His wife waited for him to pick on her. The children feared they'd hear their parents quarrelling violently again. His mother would get drawn in sometimes, but mostly she was a mute, hapless spectator. Though he refrained from assaulting anyone, he'd readily shout and smash things in his way, time and again. It was enough to scare the family into silence.

Then, thrown to the other extreme of guilt and remorse, he would pop pills to wake himself out of his hangover, to be back at work again. His resolve of not drinking, each day, would melt into nothingness by afternoon, when he couldn't wait to get home to his drink. The same scenes would invariably play out again and again.

PK knew that he was out of control. He was a bright man and could see he was self-destructing. His dependence added to his frustration, to his anger, which, in turn, further fed his anguish and rage. Each time his resolve to stop drinking failed, his helplessness increased. He drugged himself more, and lashed out harder, at those vulnerable around him—his family and his subordinate staff. Those who could leave, did. The others bore the brunt. He was caught in a wheel of acute despair, the hub of which he was unable, or unwilling, to put his finger on. He rode on its momentum, faster and faster, feeding and fighting it with extreme emotion, subconsciously waiting for something to snap. One day, he collapsed.

The doctors gave him an ultimatum. Stop drinking or die. His liver was affected, both by the alcohol and the unlimited sweetmeats he consumed. His intestines were in a mess owing to the cocktail of medicines he was mindlessly taking to keep himself alert and awake. His kidneys and pancreas were underperforming. Only age was on his side. He was not yet 40, and could pull through.

His family watched over him constantly. One drink and he could fall back. His eldest daughter, now nearly 15, was instrumental in his recuperation. She'd grown up sombre from his doings at home, numb with time to his violent and uncontrollable side. She saw him as a victim of his own helplessness and took charge of the situation. Her younger sister, 13, was withdrawn and kept out of everybody's way. Her brother, the youngest of them all, still only eight, seemed mostly unaffected by the grimness of things. The women doted on the boy, and so he'd kept his cheer so far. PK's wife had issues of her own.

From the time she'd married him, PK's wife felt out of depth. He seemed disinterested in her. Though the marriage was consummated, it seemed more like an obligation that he was fulfilling. She'd often felt dissatisfied, even neglected. Neither her husband, nor she talked about it to each other. For a woman to speak up about sex was unacceptable and considered indecent, permitted only to a woman of 'low character'.

PK's mother held his wife responsible for the things that had gone wrong. It was the woman's fault that the man was unhappy. Never a confident woman, PK's wife was driven to greater confusion and despair.

Nonetheless, she tended to her husband, with a wish to end their troubles. He was making an effort, and she supported him, carefully supervising his diet and lifestyle. He began spending more time with his children. After school, they would land up at his office, where he'd consult and liaison for businesses on export processes. They'd finish their homework, while he would meet clients or make calls. He'd take them for an evening treat later on the way back home. Slowly, a sense of positivity began to descend on him.

He found colleagues to play golf with. Waking up early, eating right and keeping his head clear of drunkenness and prescription drugs, gave him a new lease of life. Over the next seven years, he redefined his life, and threw himself, once again, in work and duty.

Then, a young intern joined his business for a brief while. In his early 20s, the man was effeminate, with a soft, affected manner of speaking. He'd grown up to believe he was different, and that constant thought had shaped his mind. He always offered a different take on things, sometimes without reason or logic to back it up. It seemed a quirk, a reaction to things that ran deeper.

PK sought the intern out on all matters, taking him to every meeting. Work hours extended to weekends. He invited the young man home, to hang around or to take a walk with him.

The family noticed a change in PK. His responses were less distraught. He seemed more relaxed and spontaneous than before, and so his family let their guard down. This period was brief though.

The internship drew abruptly to an end. The young man had

applied for a job abroad, and all clearances had come through. Soon after he left, PK took to the bottle. This time was worse than before. He drank with vengeance, and wreaked havoc on everyone within reach. His wife withdrew in alarm. His second daughter displayed symptoms of manic depression. His son seemed confused and helpless. PK's mother had died a few months earlier. His elder daughter, married and settled in another town, tried to hold things together, but had an unsupportive husband and in-laws, who put their needs first. She was torn between the two and couldn't be more present at home.

Within a year and a half, suffering and pathetic in temperament, PK was gone. He was 49.

Sexuality is a potent determinant for mental health. Whether a person is heterosexual or non-heterosexual (lesbian, gay, bisexual, pansexual), these are leanings that when suppressed (consciously) or repressed, can cause deep mental anguish in ways that are difficult to ascertain. The opportunity for people to openly identify with their sexual preferences and express them depends significantly on the environment they live in, on what is permissible or not. For non-heterosexual persons, the status assigned to them—legal and societal—matters significantly.

'In India, where homosexuality was legally considered a crime until 2018, gay people were often subjected to the threat or the reality of constant harassment,' says Rishi Talwar[8], a young psychologist. 'Crimes against the LGBTQ[9] community could go unreported because the very first revelation could put the victim in jail for 10 years. That was the law until recently. They were easy targets for blackmail and extortion. Cases of trauma that originate from this are ample.'

Trauma, a murderous death or rape, are not uncommon occurrences for LGBTQ+ people, who live in a homophobic society. Women who prefer women, but are forced to marry men as the only permissible societal sexual relationship, can experience a lifetime of sexual discomfort or even marital rape. I recall reading about a homophobic incident several years ago in which, a young man hacked his 35-year-old aunt and her roommate to death, in a slum colony on the outskirts of Delhi. His motive: they were lesbians and deserved death. The man was never arrested. 'That was an extreme case, but in general, cishet (heterosexual) men do not like lesbian women,' KD, a gay woman in her 30s, opines. 'The implication is that a lesbian woman does not need a man, and that she is unavailable to them. The men don't like that. It threatens their sense of supremacy.'

In other innumerable incidents, men have hacked or shot women to death for 'spurning their advances'. Though these may have been heterosexual women uninterested in the man in question, the fact that most women have little option to choose their partner is reiterated through fear, violence and the mechanism of shame.

A woman who may be asexual and single is frequently treated with disdain and even suspicion. Regardless of the fact that *she* may not be interested in any sexual alliance, the male and female keepers of structure often consider her a threat. 'Will she have eyes for my husband? Will my husband be interested in her? Why is she single?' are the underlying insecurities.

Men who prefer men can experience a lifetime of denial and dissatisfaction. A deep sense of conflict can pervade their inner lives, since most are primed to perpetuate patriarchal hegemony, with emphasis on having a son. Conditioned to express angst aggressively, their frustration can directly and violently affect the lives of their parents, wives, children and other close associates, besides their own, as in PK's case.

'The sign that any other sexual leaning apart from heterosexuality is taboo or abnormal comes through various media, including self-professed godmen, who proclaim to cure you of this "disease",' says Talwar. 'For a young boy or girl, trying to confront his or her preferences, the first point is how the immediate community feels about it or reacts to it. It starts with family and relatives, close or distant. They tend to make fun of gay people. Popular cinema has done it for years. A gay man is usually a comic subject or a criminal. In short, they belong to an abnormal group. The child feels that this is unacceptable and may not be able to muster the courage to declare his or her leanings and come out, if he is gay.'

'Parents sometimes believe that this is "a choice". One young man who gathered courage and clarity to state his homosexual preference to his parents, was asked, "Why are you choosing this? Why don't you make it work with a woman?" Another reaction is to consider this an experimental phase, where the child has been experimenting for a bit, and now should get serious, marry well and settle down to having a family,' says Talwar.

There is a movement towards change, though. In May 2015, Padma Iyer, the mother of gay activist Harish Iyer, placed a matrimonial advertisement in the papers, looking for a 'well-placed, animal-loving, vegetarian groom for my son'. She made headlines. In June 2015, Anouk, a popular wear brand, released an online advertisement[10] depicting a lesbian couple, under their 'Bold and Beautiful' series.[11] The video went viral, pushing sexual boundaries to new ground where live-in relationships are still treated with shock in most parts of the country.

The advertisement pushed a growing narrative. Celebrities from fashion and film live gay lives. The Pride parade, first held in 1999 with 15 people in attendance, now takes place in over 20 cities with thousands of participants. The web is allowing people to connect with others and find comfort in similarity, without necessarily having to reveal their identities. 'It's a relief,' says AS, a gay man, in his 20s, about being able to connect with others on the internet. 'It's almost cathartic in knowing that you are understood and accepted.' But this is true for groups that are homophobic as well. They too are finding support and add to the extremity of the dialogue around LGBTQ+ or matters of sexuality in general. 'I don't think I can share the truth of being gay with my family,' says AS. 'They would freak out. I know that. It is tough. Real relationships matter, especially close and intimate ones. The need to pretend or cover up is very stressful.'

Once again, the limited definition of 'normal' in terms of sexuality expands the definition of abnormal. Anything that differs and posits another way of life is mostly feared and resisted.

SENSUALITY

At an HIV-AIDS awareness event in New Delhi in 2007, Bollywood actress Shilpa Shetty led the Hollywood actor Richard Gere by the hand onto the stage. As she greeted the audience, Gere kissed her hand, embraced her, and then surprised her by bending her over in a dramatic dance pose, kissing her several times. Despite his gallant bow to her as she recovered her balance, the incident spurred outrage. Television channels replayed the incident as effigies of Gere and posters of Shetty were burnt in protests across six cities.

Protesters accused Gere of taking liberties with an Indian woman 'who was not even his wife' and insulting Indian culture. Shetty was accused for not doing anything to stop him. Apologies were demanded. A court in Rajasthan issued arrests warrants for both (later dismissed by the Supreme Court) for violating India's strict anti-obscenity laws.

Shetty had been taken by surprise when Gere had held her. She was, in fact, somewhat embarrassed by his flamboyant gesture. 'That was a bit much,' she confessed to the audience, just as he'd let her go. This fact, however, was overlooked. When an incident of a sexual or sensual nature occurs, however slight or serious, the woman finds herself bearing the brunt of blame. Such reactions usually stem from the fear discussed earlier. Rather than a cause for celebration of beauty and spirit, a confident woman is a hazard to the system and order of patriarchy. She may defy the assigned roles of diffident wife and sacrificing mother. She may become a role model and upset channels of control. Women have to be contained; their sensuality suppressed, covertly and overtly, is the undertone of the dominant narrative.

The effect can translate insidiously into low self-esteem, a prominent marker for major depression and anxiety, and other personality-related disorders. A woman is expected to prepare herself for marriage as the one main event of her life. Her grooming should be in pursuance of a good groom. Once that is accomplished, and especially once she's had children, little outward reason supposedly remains for her to seem attractive. A woman who takes pride in her appearance may call for unwarranted attention and comments. If she is attractive, she must be demure in manner and speech. Or else, her morality is brought into question. That a woman can dress up as an expression of her taste or preference, for her own sake, is a fact not easily understood by most in society.

Another cause that affects a woman's sensuality adversely is a dampened spirit. Years of adhering to a specified role of domesticity, leaves her constrained in thought and expression. Economically and physically restricted and dependent on the system, she may have no other place to go to and, often, have no real choices. In larger families, her privacy is compromised from the start. Intimate moments with her spouse are noted and often spoken about by other members, among other personal and private matters. 'Isn't it time for Riti to have another child?' a neighbour asked Riti's mother-in-law over a walk. 'They are going to Singapore in August, that's when they are planning one,' came the answer. With little or no sense of privacy, personal expression or growth, the one way for a woman to keep her happiness, or a semblance of it, is to give in to her circumstances and their demands.

It is thus common for a lot of Indian women to seem older in body and mind than their years, after marriage. It may come from a reticent letting go, from a disconnect with things that are sensually celebratory. This affects the relationship with the spouse as well. A man may find his wife an unwilling partner in sexual intimacy, from the fact that she may feel so out of it.

On the other hand, if women do express their desires, it leads to rage, like in the case of MT and BT, cited earlier. 'I'm flooded with such cases,' says Dr Pulkit Sharma[12], psychotherapist and author. 'The husbands are furious about the fact that the women are expressing their sexual dissatisfaction with them. "Can I live with such a forward-looking woman?" is the man's dilemma. These are educated men, often well-travelled, but those who've followed the script, and expect their family lives to fit the mould of "societal normalcy" as defined by their parents. They are often not prepared for change,' says Dr Sharma.

Change is creeping in, though. In an advertisement on television (for Tata Docomo), a teenage boy sits near his desktop when his father enters the room.[13] 'You're almost 16 today,' he tells his son. The boy shrugs. 'I think we should talk about... girls?' says the dad, somewhat embarrassed. The boy shrugs. 'Ya sure, Dad,' he says nonchalantly, 'what do you want to know?' The man stares at his son, surprised at the boy's informed stance, and struck by his own inhibitions.

Once again, the internet is leading to significant social change, as also to extreme upheaval. Three young women confronted a volunteer working on sexual literacy in an urban slum with a video. Their husbands were friends and had sent their wives pornographic content with a forced fetish. They were demanding the women to comply. 'What *is* this, didi?' the women asked, stunned with disbelief.

Such incidents cut across economic class or strata, where a wife is confronted with a demand she is unable to bring herself to comply with. Content shared and demanded could be of consensual porn or of non-consensual porn, i.e., videos of grotesque and violent crime against mostly women and children, both boys and girls. The act of watching such dark content can impact and alter a person's mental and emotional balance, at times irrevocably. In a society that has traversed sexual maturity and responsibility in yet limited numbers, access to the internet with little or no checks and balances, is ripping through its social fabric.

Free Wi-Fi provided by the Indian Railways at Patna city's station a few years ago, according to a report, threw up these revelations—most number of sites surfed were pornographic sites;[14] many of the users were young boys and men who would enter within the free Wi-Fi zone and use, or misuse, the facility for hours, watching porn and other videos of sexual abuse and assault.

While watching porn may be considered a personal choice, its effects however do not necessarily remain personal and limited to the individual watching it. Graphic images and sounds of a sexual nature feed the sexual urge. Now charged, the individual looks for an outlet. Some find compliance with a partner. Yet, where repression is built within the system, this outlet can result in a forced encounter—groping at the very least, but even serious molestation, sexual abuse and assault. If two or more boys or men view such content together, elements of the mob dynamic creep in to make them feel that satisfying their sexual urge, with impunity, is in place, at whatever cost.

Public spaces are rendered unsafe, both deserted places as well as crowded ones, such as railways stations, public transport and bazaars. Young teenage girls and children are targeted the most, since several factors get in the way of them reporting abuse. Children as victims include little girls and boys.

Apart from the immediate physical harm and shock a victim experiences, the effect on the social tissue is tremendous. Victims of molestation, abuse or assault harbour a profound and deep-rooted sense of injustice. If and when expressed, it mostly translates into uncontrollable anger, debilitating depression and even suicide. If unexpressed, the injustice, as a seed, darkly imprints the psyche. It can take a lifetime to handle all what such abuse can throw up. Close associates and family members come directly into the circuit of impact. Apart from consoling and counselling a victim of abuse and assault, their sense of rage, helplessness and grief on seeing a loved one suffer such injustice, can be overwhelming. (When Nirbhaya succumbed to her injuries, her younger brother was inconsolable and visibly distraught, each time the family was in the public eye. Deeply attached to his sister, he said that the incident had left him numbed with pain.) In essence, human potential is lost in large numbers, for no reason other than an abuser's titillating urge to satisfy, or at times, to entertain himself.

New York City residents felt the seedy impact of free Wi-Fi kiosks, which were installed for people to consult maps, check weather and charge their phones. But the facility attracted people who would watch porn publicly for hours, sometimes drunk or drugged. Residents complained in 2016, and the operating company had to shut down the provision to use browsers at these kiosks.

A global city, New York's laws and law-enforcement officers are more responsive and better equipped to address such complaints. Yet, it could not deal with the unintended effects of free Wi-Fi.

In a country such as ours, where support systems are grossly inadequate, not enough is in place to deter sexual abuse, to monitor individuals with such leanings or to bring perpetrators to justice.

India, therefore, is in conflict—between what has become the rigid, unbending weight of conformism on one hand, and an abrasive, loud and inconsiderate defiance that the fury of new technology and information has unleashed, on the other. If the conventional definition of 'normal' is limited and binding, the new 'no-bounds' approach seems unsustainable as well. Each represents extremity.

While that cauldron churns, 'normal' in terms of sexuality chiefly focuses on community, family and progeny. There is so far little space for celebrating individual expression—cishet, gay or differently gendered.

FOUR

NORMAL IN MIND-SCIENCE

Since the advent of psychiatry about a hundred years ago, the question of what is normal or abnormal has formed one of its core inquiries. Defining normal would, in turn, help explain abnormal. It would determine if a patient has a disorder and needs expert intervention or not.

Modern techniques consider various paradigms. A primary model is the statistical model, which looks at what may be considered 'average' or 'mean' to define abnormal–normal. 'In the statistical norm, an average range is defined for a parameter, within which most of the population is expected to fall,' Dr Mrinal Jha, a consulting psychiatrist at VIMHANS (Vidyasagar Institute of Mental Health, Neuro & Allied Sciences), explains. 'Let's say, the average intelligence quotient (IQ) is 70 to 120. Most of the population would come between these two parameters. In this way, deviations can be picked out. Those below this range would be considered meeting the diagnosis of mental retardation, while those above it would be above average, above normal, or even geniuses.'[15]

The behavioural model looks out for behaviour that might interfere with the functioning of an individual. A person could be particular about cleanliness. However, if this need for cleanliness is a cause for great anxiety, fear and distress, then it lies beyond the range of normal. An obsession affects an individual's thoughts, to impact behaviour. It gets in the way of work and functioning, and would need expert intervention. Addictions can also significantly affect behaviour and wellness.

Shank was the young manager at a graphics studio. He was polite and attentive, unlike his contemporaries, and everyone liked him. One evening, at about 8, Shank called to say that he was in the vicinity. 'Could I collect a cheque for your work at the studio, so far?' he asked. It was an unusual request since we always settled the bill only once we were done with a project. But he insisted, collected the cheque and left.

My team and I finished the project a few days later. Shank was on leave, so we cleared our remaining account with the graphic designer, who would double up as the receptionist at times.

A week later we heard that Shank was in trouble. He'd collected cheques from various clients, opened an account with a similar name as the company he worked for, and had deposited all the money in his account. His boss had filed a police complaint and the cops were looking for him.

My colleagues and I had known Shank for three years and were shocked. Out of high school, Shank was this pleasant youngster who'd hang around looking to help and be of use. We couldn't imagine or understand what may have driven him to engage in fraud.

'He has to drink every night,' his colleague informed us. 'Once, when I refused to join him because I had work to finish, he began to weep! I was so surprised. I didn't know how to handle him, so I had a couple of drinks with him, to have him stop crying. It's a problem.'

Behaviour that is considered 'normal' is not meant to harm either the individual or others around him or her. Drinking moderately is considered normal. However, drinking to a point where the person's thoughts and actions begin to revolve around the habit makes it an addiction, even an obsession. It may grow to inflict consistent harm on the person—functionally, financially, psychologically and socially—as well as harm others around, and could then require sustained attention and intervention to break out of.

Smoking is a more commonplace example as an addiction that compromises one's standing. Colleagues have refused work opportunities that require them to travel abroad. They know that they won't be able to smoke on board, and so taking a long flight is 'out of the question'. Their choices revolve around things that do not restrict their ability to smoke when they wish to. The addiction thus limits them from performing at normal potential, with functional and financial implications.

The biomedical model measures normal through the absence of physiological or neurological pathology. The parameters test for coordination between the mind/brain and the hands, arms, fingers and feet, and speech, among other checks. Children are often checked for their psychomotor skills—their ability to throw a ball, for example. If no dysfunction exists, then all is okay.

Cognitive aspects are significant in the definition of normal. Thought patterns matter, since they impact an individual's perception of reality. Does a person's self-image match facts on the outside? Are there any gaps in accurately understanding his/her identity, resources, abilities, memories? Excess of confusion or anxiety, as well as delusions, have to be checked for.

Model theories, put simply, check for cognitive abilities, personality and behaviour, and functioning within a social context. All three together as the bio-psycho-social model looks to examine disorder and disease.

'Because it is so difficult to define what is normal, we have taken up the task of describing and defining that which is abnormal,' Dr Jha explains. 'Experienced minds working in mental health have therefore formulated, and regularly revise, a rigid set of criteria to diagnose mental illnesses. The

Diagnostic and Statistical Manual of Mental Disorders (DSM-5) classifies illnesses under the broad headings of substance abuse, psychotic illnesses, mood disorders, anxiety disorders, personality disorders, eating disorders and others. When we interview a patient, we see which category his or her illness is likely to fall under, and then see if it meets the specific criteria laid out in terms of the number of symptoms, severity of illness, duration and socio-occupational dysfunction. If symptoms fall within such criteria, then there is disorder or illness. If not, then it is considered a manifestation of normal behaviour.'

'I personally define normal by certain parameters,' says Dr Pulkit Sharma[16], psychologist and author. 'A person should view his or her self and others in stable, accurate and complex ways. He or she should be able to maintain satisfying intimate relationships, and to regulate his or her impulses to understand their effects on others around. He or she should be able to age well, accepting the changes that ageing inevitably brings with it. He or she should function with mature responsibility, and understand conventional notions of reality. The person may experience transitional symptoms but should be able to respond to and handle stress without undue difficulty.' These parameters help broadly monitor normal functioning, both for personal assessment as well as from another's point of view.

In general, 'normal' behaviour is determined through a spread of lenses and factors, in which the socio-cultural model is an influential determinant, especially for the layperson. Whatever is regarded regular and usual within the social and cultural norms of a community is loosely considered 'normal'.

Early childhood is particularly important in this context of 'designing' or socio-cultural indoctrination. Impressions at this stage are powerful and lasting, for better or for worse. Children pick cues from their environment on permissiveness, conduct, gender parity or subjugation, and interpersonal relationships. In more extreme cases, children, particularly boys, who've witnessed aggression or domestic violence at home are prone to continue the same patterns as adults. 'You think it's okay to do that, to be the way you see people around you behave,' says Manisha Amin[17], counsellor and teacher who works with children of displaced populations in London.

Since societal norms influence the perceptions of what 'normal' or 'normal behaviour' is about, this could lead to the creation of an identity from a compulsion to fit in. Such an identity is usually different from how a person really is. Discussed under Self-Presentation[18] in Social Psychology, the theory delves into how a person influences his or her image and presentation to conform to a certain image in mind, or to impress an image on an audience. Erving Goffman, the Canadian social psychologist who propounded the theory, used the metaphor of theatre to present his concept of how we change faces, or present different faces to an audience that changes through the day. One would behave differently going out with friends to a pub, as one would in the company of grandparents or at a professional meeting. Motivations for self-presentation are usually genuine and automatic, when we play various acquired roles—that of a child, parent, employer, employee, friend, confidante, mentor and so on. Role or image is also determined by culture as well as by law, which outline what may be considered 'appropriate behaviour'.

However, where ethics are compromised, self-presentation may be driven by the need for psychological manipulation—from an individual's deceitful portrayal as a victim (rather than as perpetrator), to opaque corporate jargon, with the aim to present an image other than what is real or fact.

While tradition and culture can forcefully determine image, social media as a relatively new development puts an enormous amount of pressure on the individual. The need to have a certain image—cool, 'with it', the best, 'original' and 'different', leading the perfect life and such—can cause immense strain and conflict in the psyche. The more the gap between a virtual image and the real self or resources, the greater the chance for disharmony within. Never before have little children suffered as much anxiety en masse (except in war and conflict zones) as now. Never before have adults felt as obsolete as now, by the endless pace of tech change, or through the fear of missing out. The effect on inner mechanisms is immense.

Aside from theories in modern psychology, it is imperative to consider a couple of older cues in understanding normal-abnormal. Dissecting these may offer clues for a steady and healthy normal. According to *Webster's Third New International Dictionary*, for instance, the word 'eccentric' derives its root from the Greek *ekkentros* meaning 'out of the center' (*Ek* = out of, *Kentron* = centre).

It seems to have appeared in the sixteenth century as an expression in astronomy to mean 'not having the Earth as centre'. It also meant located elsewhere than at the geometrical centre or not having the same centre, as opposed to *concentric*. Thus, 'eccentric' meant deviating and departing from the centre or from the line of a circle. With time, it moved from its original literal meaning to a metaphoric one to describe unconventional or peculiar behaviour, for a person whose conduct is quirky or atypical.

In another example, the root of the word 'health' (Proto-

Germanic *hailitho*) denotes wholeness or being hale or whole. It emphasizes physical soundness (being uninjured) as well as welfare and happiness.

Finally, the Sanskrit word for 'health', dating back one to two millennia BCE at least, is *Svāsthya* (from *Sva* or 'one's own, natural' and *Stha* or 'being centred'). *Svāsthya* therefore implies rooted at one's inner centre for physical, sensual, emotional and mental wellness.

All three concepts overlap in implying that health and normality is *wholeness*. It indicates a coming together of various systems of body, and sheaths and layers of mind and emotion. For the body to be healthy or normal, vital systems should work *together*, without undue strain or strife. Normal would suggest not only a lack of conflict, but further a sense of confluence between sheaths and within each, as well.

Thus 'normal' would be a state of fluid functioning, where the expression of mind-psyche-emotion-body and aspiration are in tandem, without the markings of intense or devitalizing inner or outer conflict.

If normal is wholeness, then within the circumference of wholeness, what is the centre? What may hinge us to it? Why is it so potent, that being 'off centre' is understood as the cause for aberrant behaviour? Is this centre a fixed, rigid point, oblivious to time-milieu and variable external circumstance, or is it dynamic?

And finally, could influences around us and the power of emotions within, to which we may be unmindful, pull at the alignment of our centring or tear into our wholeness, to cause us to unhinge?

I believe they can.

SECTION II
UNHINGE

*Nothing in life is to be feared
It is only to be understood.*

—Marie Curie
Physicist and Nobel Prize Laureate

FIVE

TRAPPED
The Depressive Abyss

Maya, 26, came to Sitaram Bhartiya Institute of Science and Research, New Delhi, with an older cousin, for counselling. She complained of fatigue, body ache, lack of concentration and confusion. She was working as a freelance copywriter for an internet firm. Of late, she had been finding it difficult to sleep and to keep up with work. She had been missing deadlines. Always good at study and work, this for her was a cause for alarm. She'd been waking up later and later, with her day starting around noon. She said that she felt ill and under rested every morning, and dull, as if her brain hadn't woken up. She had trouble making simple choices. It took her hours to decide what to wear for the day, and the task seemed overwhelming. She was unable to remember things to do in the day or the week ahead. It felt like 'one big jumble' in her head. The jumble was also from having too many thoughts 'whizzing in my brain', she said. She wanted to 'sleep all day and all week'. Her energy levels seemed to improve in the evenings, when she'd leave home and sit with her friends at a restaurant or a coffee shop, or hang out at a friend's place, usually past midnight. She dreaded the mornings and 'wanted time to stop'.

Maya lived with her parents, an older and a younger brother. The family was upper middle class, with no pressing financial concerns. She described her family as loving, and her childhood as modest and responsible. Her cousin said that lately things were strained at home. Always a quiet and amiable person, Maya had become increasingly irritable and unapproachable. She had stopped talking to her parents and would only respond to her younger brother, if he goaded her enough. To this, Maya said that she wanted to 'get away from it all'.

Through subsequent sessions of counselling, the cause for Maya's predicament began to emerge. A couple of years earlier, she had returned from completing her master's in another town. Within a week of returning home, her brother found her crying on her bed. She said nothing to him, but admitted in counselling that she had grown quietly accustomed to her own space—of taking her own decisions, of following her own rhythm of study and work, of deciding her own company and mapping her time. Here at home, she felt no sense of privacy. Everyone had an opinion not only on what she did, but on what everyone else was doing as well. Her choice to meet a friend, even, was open to familial scrutiny. While this was how things had always been at home, a process that she had once been accustomed to, now, she'd begun to feel restricted and constrained.

Maya's family was unable to acknowledge and concede to their adult daughter's wish for independent expression. They continued to take decisions on her behalf. Her brothers and parents thought of this as their assertion of love for her. To them, Maya was still the young girl, who had to be protected and directed. They had 'allowed her' to live on her own for a couple of years, and that was liberal and fair enough, they said. The next and only step on their minds was her marriage. They felt it their duty to find her a good home and husband, to make sure their daughter was 'settled in life'. The more they broached the topic with her, the more alienated she felt from them. Always pleasant to be with, she became increasingly ill-tempered and would often shout at her father and brothers to leave her alone.

Maya said she was angry with her father and two brothers for dominating her life; at her mother, for accepting this arrangement unquestioned; and most of all at her own self, for not following her instincts of taking the opportunity to work and live on her own at the end of her master's programme. Genuinely attached to her family, she knew they loved her and meant well. That prevented her from making a clean break and moving away. It also fuelled her anger, at herself, for feeling this way about her loved ones. 'They do so much for me,' she said, 'and yet I hate them!'

Conflicted within, her mind incessantly scrutinized the point at which she could've decided to do her own bidding. Time and again, she thought of how things could have been different had she explored other prospects, had she decided to stay in her town of choice. She had a good job offer after her master's and she felt she would've been happier and proactive living on her own. 'Why did this happen?' was a raging question in her mind. 'Why has this happened to *me*?'

As her mind raced, she began to freeze in her functioning. Drained by an all-consuming stream of confrontational thought in her head, she felt the need to sit or lie down, most of the time. 'My mind would be whirling in several directions at one time. It was like an unending film, constantly playing in my mind.' She would thus lie in bed, emotionally and physically overwhelmed by the crisis in her head. She thought she had to think herself through this for it to resolve. The more she thought about it, the more the past engulfed her present.

Even as she receded into a shell of her own, her anger grew at feeling her life being taken away from her. She felt betrayed. Her family had always been her anchor. Now, in conflict with them, she felt rudderless and lost. Outwardly, she grew silent and listless; inwardly, she raged.

Amongst the most talked about disorders, depression tops the list. Current estimates have it that one in every four people in India, and around the world, are susceptible to an episode of major depression at least once in their lifetime.

Symptoms include feeling constantly and abnormally low over a period of more than two to three weeks. This could build to a persistent sadness over a period of several weeks or months and a subsequent loss of interest. Usually, anger and helplessness are the dominant and underlying emotions that characterize this mood disorder. A loss of appetite or a significant increase in it, insomnia or too much sleep, continuing fatigue and the inability to concentrate are indicators of the disorder setting in.

Other physiological effects include lack of concentration, the inability to remember working details (telephone numbers, tasks at hand, to-do lists) and an overriding feeling of confusion. There occurs a resultant loss of will, pleasure and drive.

These are debilitating changes that affect normal functioning. They tend to first show up in a withdrawal from social interaction, in increasingly not wanting to engage with others. They may then interfere with the routine and ability to work, with relationships at home, and then, depending on the severity of the disorder, in the decrease and lack of personal hygiene—when a person doesn't wish to get out of bed even for the most basic functions.

What causes depression is under the scanner, more now than ever before.

The Freudian view, put simply, is that depression is anger turned inwards, when typically one is angry at close and loved ones, and is unable or unwilling to openly express anger. Anger is suppressed in expression, but continues to erupt within. The mind vacillates between blaming others and one's own self as the reason for things going wrong. It gets caught in a wheel of anger and guilt, which pervades all thinking and doing. This persistent feeling of guilt, of blaming loved ones, as well as of holding oneself responsible for all ills, overrides other emotions, especially positive ones.

From a cognitive-behavioural approach, depression is learned helplessness—the feeling that nothing can be done to bring about change of any consequence, and that all, in any case, is pointless. This stage may be reached after a particular event or episode doesn't turn out as expected—in work, in a relationship or in life—as in Maya's case.

Learned helplessness can also generate from the environment at home or at work. Usually, an excessively dominating parent, caregiver or superior can cause others to feel less proactive, less in charge of their own wishes and actions. Over time, this may lead to a sense of helplessness, when a person feels trapped at home or in a work environment, but believes nothing can be done to change the situation. A resigned sense of hopelessness and worthlessness become a way of being.

A common provocation to the onset of depression, especially in young Indian adults, is the inability of the family and community to acknowledge and accept their individuality. Where communities are strong and binding, as in Maya's case, independent-minded, able men and women tend to feel stifled. Elders of the immediate or extended family often dismiss their reason and aspiration. Age and experience are given precedence over intelligence, enthusiasm and enterprise. The desire for privacy is discouraged, and the wish to break away is often met with indignation, or regarded as disloyal to family or community.

The effect for such individuals is commonly a sense of

entrapment—of feeling forced into a situation that disregards their adulthood and their ability to take responsibility for their own selves. It is a frequent reason, in societies that enforce submission to structure and hierarchy, for depression to set in.

For this reason, depression is more common among women than in men, with twice as many women than men inclined to be susceptible. 'Women are more likely to feel stuck. They feel that they do not have control over their lives, that they do not have the resources to make the decisions they want to make, to lead their lives independently,' Dr Susan Nolen-Hoeksema, former head of psychology at Yale, had said to me in an interview.

Reactions to depression differ as well, between men and women. 'Men may experience more irritability and anger if depressed, whereas women are more likely to shut down,' says Dr Darin Dougherty[19], of the Harvard Medical College.

Experts are now looking to identify genes that may be related to depression. Depression seems to run in families, where patterns of behaviour and reactions tend to perpetuate. As a result, some individuals may be more prone to depression than others. However, no single gene seems to cause depression. Even if a person inherits a particular genetic disposition from a depressive parent, it may or may not act out in the individual.

The research so far suggests that while the genetic map may play a role in some individuals, it isn't necessarily the only, or the dominant, factor in triggering depression. Environment and experience are equally potent factors. Children may imbibe patterns of behaviour or reactions by being with a majorly depressed or a manic depressive parent. They learn from what they see. Unpleasant childhood memories—discord between parents, neglect, a feeling of abandonment, or emotional and/or physical abuse—are potent causes for depression, even later in life. The child somehow holds his or her own self responsible for what went wrong, and subsequently nurses a feeling of guilt and inferiority that contributes to low self-esteem, a forceful marker for depression. The strongest cues could thus be from the environment, especially early environments, which powerfully imprint a child's mind.

This applies to the case of the young woman, (Chapter 2: The Gender Normal), who wasn't allowed to work after marriage, by her husband and in-laws. Emotionally disturbed and agitated, mentally unprepared for a child, and physically under strain and stress, she delivered a baby girl, a child of 11 at the time of this interview.

Being around a parent who still nurses resentment from the past and silently holds the marriage and child responsible for her predicament, the girl seems to have picked up on those cues. Uncommunicative, she is inhibited in articulating her thoughts, readily, both at school and at home. Instead, she abounds in tantrums and vocal outbursts, when expressing irritability or anger. Socially awkward, she resists meeting new people, especially when guests visit. Her moods are unpredictable. As a child of five or six, she was inclined to cry often, sometimes a few times a day. She would hide herself under the bed or a table, especially if a demand was rejected. Now, at 11, she usually seems sullen.

In another instance, Bala, 32, came to a clinical facility with his mother and wife, after he'd attempted suicide. Until a year prior to this episode, he'd worked for a few years as the manager of a small firm in a southern metropolis. He was reliable, responsible and respected at work. A good student at school and university, he'd worked his way up in the firm to be appointed the second-in-command at their local office. On the personal front, he'd been married for eight years. His wife was a homemaker, taking care of him, their two children, and his mother, who lived with them. The family, from a middle-income group, was able to live comfortably.

Bala was accustomed to a routine. He would awaken around 6 a.m., exercise for half an hour and leave for work by 8 a.m. One morning, he said he was not feeling too well. He complained of fatigue and felt he hadn't slept well. Over the next three weeks, his aches and pains seemed to increase in intensity. He began to get out of bed late and abandoned his morning routine of stretches. He'd leave for work an hour or so later than usual, which was okay, since he was permitted flexible hours.

A couple of weeks later, his wife found him sobbing in bed. He said he'd been feeling low and was not prepared to go to work. She calmed him down and though he went to work, this scene became a daily occurrence over the next few weeks. She'd wake up to him sobbing and would then spend the next few hours reassuring him that all was okay. He would go to work reluctantly and would then call his wife a few times a day, saying he wasn't able to focus and wished to come back home. By evening, however, he felt his spirits lift a little.

After a month, he refused to get out of bed altogether. His wife's pleas were to no avail. He said his body was breaking and he felt devoid of all energy. He had no inclination or will to go to work or do anything else. His wife suggested a visit to his former psychiatrist. A couple of years earlier, Bala had experienced a bout of moderate depression that had lasted a few months. Though he'd been asymptomatic in the interim years, it seemed another episode was unfolding.

The doctor prescribed medicines, which he monitored and changed over the next three months. Bala initially took time off from work and refused to interact with anyone from his office. At home too, he refused to speak with his wife and mother, or with anyone from amongst his circle of friends. If his friends dropped by to look him up, he would refuse to come out of his room to meet with them.

Then, in the following weeks, he reported a slight improvement in his mood and appetite and got back to work, though hesitatingly. A few weeks later, he felt better and resumed part of his earlier routine. His appetite and sleep improved. Though he was able to put in a full day at work, he wouldn't socialize with friends in the evenings, as he had done earlier.

A couple of months into his medication, he once again complained about feeling extremely low. He was continuing with the prescribed drugs, but he said he didn't believe this medication could help him any more. He said he felt exhausted and would cry in his wife's presence. He felt his depression was worsening and there was nothing that could help him out of it. He said he did not wish to continue working; it was pointless. On a couple of occasions earlier, he'd called up his boss and offered his resignation. He would tell his boss that he was of no use to the firm any more. Then he would pace all day at home, overcome with worry about who would fend for his family, and the next day, he would call his boss to ask for his job back again. This time, however, he adamantly quit work. He told his wife that there was 'nothing left in his future'.

He was sleeping four hours at night and would awaken early. He would cry under the covers and would refuse to get out of bed for most of the day. He would sit in front of the TV, unwilling to interact with his mother or wife. His appetite diminished drastically and he worried about it incessantly. He thought his depression would worsen if he lost weight. He weighed himself a few times a day. Though he felt no inclination to eat, he'd force himself to. He looked at the caloric chart for various dishes on the internet and would carefully chart out what he had to eat. If his daugher would pick from his plate, he would throw a fit, telling them that this would disrupt his calculations and that they would be the cause for his depression to worsen. He spent a significant amount of time doing this, but did not feel that it was unusual in any way. His personal hygiene began to suffer and he would take a shower once in two to three days.

In the meanwhile, his wife had a fall and broke her ankle. Bala, however, declined to go to the hospital with her. He said he was of no use to her or to anybody. She had to call her brother to take her instead. This was in stark contrast to how he had been earlier, when he typically was the person to take charge of a situation.

When he refused to see the doctor, his mother decided to take him to a healer. On the way, he and his wife argued about his state of mind. She told him that he was so involved with his own self that her worries and condition meant nothing to him. This apparently proved to be the last straw for him. He shut up all evening and, at night, left home when everyone was asleep. He took the first bus to a town several hours away. He bought paper and a pen and wrote a suicide note, in which he said his family should not be held responsible for his death. It was before dawn. He banged at the shutters of a courier service, until the attendant opened up. The man refused to take the letter. Bala walked to a bridge, placed his wallet and the letter on the side of the bridge, and jumped off.

The bridge, however, was infamous for suicides. A police team had been deployed round the clock to watch for people jumping off. This team spotted Bala and pulled him out almost immediately. They found his wallet and letter, and from the address mentioned on it, were able to contact the family.

The doctor who examined Bala noted that there was no perceptive abnormality, that his memory was intact, as was his general fund of knowledge. He knew who the prime minister of the country was and other general social-historical-political facts.

When he was asked what was bothering him, he said, 'I want to be left alone. There's nothing in the future for me. I used to be very respected at work, now I'm of no use to anyone. My wife informed my relatives and friends of my disorder: whatever little respect was left at home, that too is gone. No one can help me—no doctor, no medicines, no one. I'm a sensitive man. I feel such grief, and worry—it's best if all this would come to an end. No one would believe that here is the same man who would hang around with his friends until midnight, sipping beer.'

His insight into his own predicament was clear as well. 'I'm depressed,' he said. 'This disorder is not akin to a cold and cough, that I may be rid of it. I suffer from the tension at home. I'm sensitive, but my wife picks a fight with me for little things. It upsets me and I feel aggrieved, disturbed and depressed.'

Neurologists see the cause of depression as a chemical imbalance in the brain—a drop in the level of certain neurotransmitters that otherwise help neurons to communicate effectively and smoothly with each other. These biochemicals help relay messages and build coherent thought, regulate mood and our sense of pleasure. When these biochemicals are out of balance, usually with too little of them going around, the result is a loss of pleasure, a loss of drive and will.

For long, there has been debate whether this drop in neurotransmitters is a cause or an *effect* of depression. It probably works both ways; for some, it may be a cause of depression—an inherently low level of dopamine or serotonin may make individuals prone to being moody and blue; in others, it may be an effect of depression. Because their minds are raging, they use more of these chemicals than the brain can produce and hence, there is a drop in their levels.

Which is why modern therapy, in addition to mood-altering prescription drugs (under consultation of a psychiatrist), is increasingly turning to include counselling and psychotherapy, with psychologists as part of treatment. While specific drugs can lift the level of neurotransmitters so that the individual has some support to function again, it is important to address how the mind is working, what it is thinking and why. Working through the issues of the psyche is equally the key, if not more, as are circumstances and environs, which leave deep and lasting impressions on the psyche.

A closer examination of Bala's interpersonal relationships revealed that he was close to his parents since childhood, and was equally fond of his younger siblings, who were both married. But, from early on in the marriage, his relationship with his wife had been strained. According to his wife, Bala cared for her and always provided for her, but they often argued over petty issues. And although these arguments were generally resolved in a few hours, there were instances when he'd felt so frustrated that he'd forced his wife to leave the house. Their parents had to intervene to reconcile the two.

While there seemed no immediate precipitating factor that could have triggered his depression, it was apparent that Bala had been nursing resentment and anger from his relationship with his wife. Her upbringing seems to have been more constrained than his, both financially and socially. She found his hanging out with friends wasteful. On his part, Bala may have felt that she was constraining him, his expression and his will to live life. His demeanour reflected that there was no point in reasoning with her, since her limited education and exposure were at the root of her lack of understanding, and that there was nothing he could do about it. He obviously felt bound to her, as it was his responsibility and duty to look after her and their children.

Clearly, Bala felt locked into circumstances beyond his power, circumstances that he resented and even despised at times. His sense of wellness seems to have come from a feeling of reaching out—to learn, to discover, to live, within the resources of a middle-income upbringing. He evidently expected life to be that journey and to have a companion who would share and enjoy the things he did. His frustration and helplessness may have mounted when that turned out differently. His two bouts of depression, one major, one severe were palpably rooted in his sense of feeling trapped.

A sense of entrapment often underlies bouts of depression. To believe that one may not have real choices, or any choice for that matter, cleaves into a sense of hope and vigour, and into one's power to affect change. While one is aggrieved and bewildered within, innate layers are breached.

SIX

BREACH

How does it *feel* to be depressed? What pulls and pushes within, to cause us such melancholia? What is the load that we bear to make all things seem so desolate? Is it just the mind gone awry, or could it run through and through, piercing what lies at the heart of our wellness?

Herein lie traces of the usual trajectory.

We are forward-looking beings, constantly anticipating the next thing that will interest us—the next day, the next meeting, the next meal, the next cup of coffee, the next outcome from our work, the next event in our lives. We are happiest when we are in flow with this movement, ahead.

When, however, our flow is seriously interrupted, we feel an intrusion. We begin to question this interruption—what or who may have caused it and why things did not go the way we think they should have. Some of us may move on after a while; others may remain at this point of intrusion, mentally and emotionally questioning and analysing it, over and over again.

The more the sense of flow prior to the incident, the greater the reaction to this perceived interference. The mind is thrown into overdrive, looking for cause to blame. All energy is directed and expended in trying to unravel why this intrusion may have happened and how it may have been avoided. That throws up several emotions, mostly disappointment, hurt, anger, blame and frustration, simultaneously.

This implosion of thought and emotion unsettles the body. The mind, overworked and agitated, is unable to rest. Sleep is usually the first to be impacted. The result is fatigue, which builds into primary systems of the body. As days pass, one is not in rhythm with time any more, neither in awareness nor in functioning. With the mind still whizzing, the body out of whack and the emotional gaze fixed at the point of intrusion, the person reaches a point where he/she is hopelessly unprepared to face the day.

Depression is therefore often understood as the 'freeze response'. It stands apart from the fight-or-flight response.

Fight or flight is an evolutionary response designed to protect us from danger. When under threat, the sympathetic nervous system kicks in to make us fight or flee the threat. It pumps the body with hormones. The heart's rate increases, pupils dilate and adrenaline gushes into our blood to flush our limbs with strength. We need to feel strong in our hands and legs to either fight the danger or to run away from it. Other bodily systems are put on hold.

In depression, however, we neither fight nor flee clearly, but rather freeze in our functioning. Overwhelmed by thoughts, by uncontrollable emotional currents that also bear out as bodily fatigue, we tend to shut down in our relation with time and people, in the present.

A Breach in the Vital

Even beyond the freeze response, depression is a rift in the vital, a breach in its calm cohesion. The vital here is a fundamental layer (or layers) that inherently spouts stability and positivity. It is the fount for life energy. Our survival instinct is aligned with the vital. So is rhythm, in my view.

When a series of extreme emotional reactions trigger, they have the force to run deep, to distress, in turn, the components of the vital layers of the body and psyche. Together, they pull at and tear into our feeling of stability and wellness.

Time

The first component ruptured is our sense of time. We are torn between the present moment and that phase or point in the past when we perceived an intrusion. This intrusion could have been weeks, months or years ago, but with each passing day, the gap between the present and the point of unrest feels exponentially heavier.

Attention is powerfully drawn to the past, and so the present becomes a blur. Time, unaccounted for in the now and in the ever-increasing gap, becomes burdensome.

As the backlog builds, the gap gathers more weight. Anxiety arises and escalates, with each passing moment, from things that are unprocessed. Not only is the point of intrusion unprocessed, but also all that has transpired since. It remains unaddressed, quite like an unending pile of clothes that need ironing. One that has a burn and a tear in it consumes our attention, while a fresh load keeps piling up with each passing day. The load of the backlog begins to overwhelm us and so an aware flow with the present is ever more of a struggle.

Torn between the past and the blur of the present, our inherent alignment with the movement of time is ruptured, and forward momentum is blown asunder.

A frequent refrain of those suffering from depression is thus for time to stop. Maya articulated it; Bala acted upon it in his bid to take his own life. The pressure from the passing of time translates to 'the world is passing me by' and the corollary to that is 'I'm falling behind' and further, 'I will never catch up.' An acute sense of loss for time and opportunity usually flags the process of depression.

Emotions

Next, an emotional upheaval occurs, alongside.

Disappointment, from feeling let down at the point of intrusion, imbues all thought and action. 'Had I done this differently, I would've been happier' is a constant thought.

Self-blame is common and persistent. '*I* should have done that and not this. It's *my* fault. I should have said no.'

If those responsible for the point/event of intrusion are loved ones, then blame increases many fold. 'How could they do this to me?' spikes indignation, anger, and even hate. That provokes rebellion and then, guilt, for feeling so vehemently against close and loved ones. 'I'm awful and selfish to think badly of them. They love me.'

Yet, a pervading sense of injustice underscores most other feelings. It extends outward as well. Injustice is perceived everywhere and in everything. It adds up manifold to build to a choking sense of despair.

Blame and love, rebellion and guilt, despair and yet hope for things to settle, pull to opposing extremes.

A sense of cohesion in the emotional fabric is ripped apart.

Mind

While emotions are split, the mind, too, is pulled apart. 'Why did this happen to me?' is a buzzer that throws the mind into a spin.

A Pandora's box opens at this juncture, throwing up negative memories from various stages of life. Perceived failures at work, in university or school, unpleasant incidents from childhood—a sense of neglect, violence witnessed or experienced, bullying or abuse of any kind at any stage—all begin to surface, by and by. The mind actively seeks them, almost, in a bid to unravel the *why* of intrusion.

Further, because anger and disappointment are driving the mind, it digs for negative experiences actively. Many disconsolate instances, real and assumed, surface simultaneously. Each thought-memory-impulse pulls intensely to its own trajectory, like horses pulling randomly in different directions. The mind's presence is shredded.

A fabled Indian metaphor in context is the chariot analogy, where the components of a chariot in motion correspond to the various sheaths that make us up. The chariot itself is the body. Its five horses signify our five senses—touch, taste, smell, hearing and sight. The reins of the horses denote *Manas*, or mind, or more appropriately, attention. The charioteer signifies aware intellect or intelligent will. The reins of attention are in his or her hand. He or she has the power to control attention and, in turn, rein in the senses. Finally, behind the charioteer, the ultimate rider is the conscience, seated and watching over the intellect-charioteer (as a passenger-owner seated in the back seat may watch over the chauffeur of a car. The chauffeur is at his or her best because he or she is being monitored).

Interestingly, in depression, one feels rudderless, like a chariot without a functioning charioteer. With no charioteer, the mind-reins are free and loose, and are pulled in several different directions simultaneously by five unbridled senses or horses. The conscience (or consciousness if you wish) is bewildered at this floundering. It is witness to all that which is happening. 'What *is* this? This is not *me*; this is not how I know myself' it says, trying to get a grasp of things now out of hand. The intellect-charioteer, still in the seat, is unresponsive. The chariot is out of control.

Such unresponsiveness is true for the functioning of the brain in depression. While one mechanism of the brain is overworked, another faculty is dulled. Stridently engaged in retrieving unresolved memories, the brain's apparatus is therefore weaker in forming new, positive ones.

The intellect is consumed and congealed at a point or phase in the past. It is unresponsive to the present. Further, the clamour and noise of an unbridled mind cause current situational awareness to decline. Concentration is affected. To recall and carry out small tasks in the now is a strain.

Apart from pain felt intensely, the present is not vivid enough to keep us wholly in the moment. (This is probably one reason why those suffering depression are often substance abusers. It is an extreme measure to spike interest in the present and to feel alive, even if momentarily. It allows the user to have something to look forward to, however destructive. The will towards self-destruction is alive and active. It is an extreme form of protest, often from wanting to punish those who love us but have wronged us.)

Absorbed in the past and muted in the presence, there is a split between attention and action. Awareness is sluggish, a step or more behind the action, in time. A task is carried out without thinking, without being truly with it.

In effect, one begins to feel dazed, overwhelmed, confused and helpless.

Body

Further, a tear in mechanisms of brain-mind-emotion affects the body's intricate balance in the way it holds and strings systems together.

With the mind pulled apart by several strains of thought and the emotional plane at an extreme pitch, the nervous system overworks. It is driven to support the mind's working that, in turn, prods, analyses, reacts, concludes, despairs and blames, all together. One wheel of thought turns another and another.

Neurons fire at great speed, incited mostly by anger. Neuronal signals collide, with almost nothing finding a point of positive resolve or rest. The nervous system, under intense pressure, is overwhelmed.

The result is confusion, as well as anxiety, in mind and body. Such an onslaught, in turn, affects sleep.

The gut, with its plethora of neurons, is thrown into anxious disarray. Enzyme production (which includes serotonin and dopamine) as well as gut motor function is compromised, as is its power to absorb. That, in turn, directly affects levels of nourishment and energy.

The breath alters, now shorter and shallower, lacking energy that is powerfully consumed by the mind and its thoughts, as well as from a decrease in stamina.

Vital systems of the body are similarly depleted in their ready vigour. Sloth builds. The body feels strained to lift its own weight. Posture begins to change, energy levels drop and gait slows, from actual physiological tiredness as well as from a deepening sense of helplessness.

An inexplicable heaviness suffuses different parts of the body, making it seem unresponsive. It can take hours to get out of bed, even though the mind is screaming instructions to do so.

Physiological equilibrium is splintered causing more emotional and mental stress, from not being in control of something as fundamental as one's body. This is one reason why depression commonly afflicts older people, frail in health. It stems from a loss of control over an irreversibly ageing body and mind, which signal that nothing will be how it was in the past, again.

For people diagnosed with chronic illness, at any age, the experience is similar—a sense of dejected bewilderment, that something is out of whack and may never be fixed the way it was. It leads to uncertainty, from not knowing how the body will be the next month, the next week, the next day or in a few hours, even. It holds one back from committing to anything. Anxiety underscores every thought. The future is tentative and takes on shades of bleakness.

Further, there is grief, for an unscathed self—for how one may have been before the intrusion, before the illness, before the event; how one may have been without this interruption. Grief heightens at feeling wronged, and deepens, from an irrevocable sense of loss.

The Feeling

Irrespective of age, this is what underlies depression—an acute sense of loss that intensifies with each tear in varied layers.

A loss of control over mind and body leads to a loss of confidence. Confidence is the ability to cope in the present moment. (It is your trust in yourself in the present.) With the body and mind doing their own thing, one is unsure of how one may fare in this moment, in the task at hand, whether one can deal with what comes next. All action, however small and mundane, is wrought with growing anxiety. The more anxious one is, the more the loss in confidence.

Such insecurity builds over an already prevalent sense of lost time—of not being able to catch up, of having lost out on opportunity and life. 'I'm a waste, a failure' is a quick, ready and repetitive thought. It is a belief that ruptures hope, each time. It pulls inwards and away from engaging with life.

The mind—distressed, confused and dejected—despairs at everything. All seems hopeless, pointless and futile—all result and, therefore, all effort. There seems little or no point in trying. Gloom pervades—deep and dark, as inner layers suffer an uncontrollable sinking into darkness, into an abyss—with no light, no hope, no future. Ever.

The vital layer—of faith-hope-stability, of rest and revival, deep within—is breached.

SEVEN

INTRUSION
Point and Plane

An intrusion is an event or incident that interferes with our flow ahead. It is a point of deep disappointment or dejection, so much so that it forcefully pulls attention to itself and disrupts onward momentum. It consumes vital energy from many folds of body, mind and psyche, to tear into our inherent sense of wellness.

Could one specific happening cause such commotion within, or could such disturbance build layer upon layer through time? Would the intrusion bear out more heavily were it to trace its beginnings to early imprints in childhood? Do early impressions matter and to what extent?

Consider KD's case to begin with.

KD was cruising. At 56, he ran a small, established business, to amply provide for the needs and demands of his immediate family, i.e., his wife and a grown-up son. Two daughters were married and settled. His work, through the years, had taken him to different parts of the country. His wife of 30 years, demure and the perennial homemaker, preferred the sanctity of routine, giving the home and family her all. His friends and relatives regarded KD a success, a man who had grown from a conservative and constrained economic stratum to have it all—a stable family, a profitable business and a penchant for life. He met with friends a couple of times a week, sometimes buying drinks for everyone. Though not garrulous, he nonetheless displayed an occasional brashness. He would intrude into conversations, bursting into comment, awkwardly at times. He wore the conscious confidence of a man who felt he knew, and could navigate, the ways of the world.

It all seemed fine, until his son met with a bike accident. The young man suffered a broken arm and ribs and though shaken, was soon out of danger. As he recuperated, KD began to seem afflicted. He fell quiet and appeared anxious and stressed, more than usual. The family attributed the mishap as the cause for the change in his demeanour. Even as his son recovered well over the next eight weeks, KD's silence grew. He would sit with his family or with visiting relatives but wouldn't speak much. He seemed distracted and disinterested. His wife and son thought he was concerned about what had been an unexpected spike in medical expenses and about the pressures it put on his work. They thought he would soon be back to his normal self.

In the coming weeks, however, KD complained of weakness and severe body ache. His gait slackened, and he became lethargic. Though he continued to go to work, his interaction both at home and work was minimal. He would wake up crying at night and would watch religious shows on the television. His wife and son, appalled at this drastic change within a span of months from the accident, would try and coax him to talk. 'Leave me alone,' he'd say tiredly, 'I'm done!' Any attempt to make him explain his stance would lead to greater withdrawal.

Several doctors were consulted, some coming home to check on him. No known cause was found for the pain he complained of all over his body. As the weeks went past, it got worse. His appetite reduced drastically, as did his weight, his clothes loosely hanging on his frame. He would lie in bed all day, and began to skip work.

One day, his son sat by his bedside and refused to leave until his father told him what was wrong. KD remained stone silent through his son's persistent questioning. Then, at one point, he sat up suddenly, and unexpectedly struck the young man across the face. Before the boy could react, KD flung whatever he could find in reach, smashing things across the floor. His wife came rushing in, startled at the commotion. As she ran to constrain him, he hit out at her, punching her in the chest. She doubled up in pain. The son threw himself at his father, and KD fell limp, wailing and weeping all at once. The family realized he was mentally disturbed. He needed help.

The psychiatrist prescribed antidepressants. For a couple of weeks, KD complied. He couldn't shake off his family, who watched over him. But then he adamantly stopped the medication. He ate frugally and sporadically. His personal hygiene suffered for days at a time. He became forgetful and unmindful of dates and names. He refused to do anything, meet anyone or go anywhere.

Then one day, he slit his wrists. The cuts weren't deep, but it appalled his family. They took him to the hospital. On his return, he tried to hang himself. The househelp spotted him and raised an alarm. A week later, he swallowed all his medication. This time, the family took him to the hospital for a longer, more sustained spell of treatment.

The therapy sessions were also a confession; KD insisted on his family's presence. He admitted to stealing and being indecent with other women. Significant facts for him were that he had begun smoking as a teen, with friends. Soon, he smoked cannabis. He knew it was something that he would get thrashed and thrown out of his house for, but he liked the fact that he was doing things on the sly. He began to steal money from home, whenever he could. He needed the money for his cigarettes and cannabis and to hang out with friends. At 18, he tried alcohol.

He began drinking a few times a week with friends. Married at 25, he thought he would quit these addictions. Unable to abstain, he began drinking alone at home, several times a week. He confessed that there were times when he and his friends spoke indecently to women who were alone. The first time he groped a woman was in a bus. It was crowded and she was getting off. It left him feeling nervous, but gave him a sense of power, and something to boast about to his friends. He did it again and again, and didn't think much about it. Subsequently, he cheated on his wife, several times.

Now, he was repenting. He shouldn't have indulged. His health had suffered. He had lost most of his teeth. He had lost out on several opportunities to do better for himself and his family because of his addictions. He needed to go to hell for what he had done. He was being punished. His son's accident had proven it to him. His children were good children. Their mother had done well with them. His son was suffering for his misdemeanours. He did not want him to suffer for his sins. Everything had turned against him. Nothing was right any more. Nothing could help him. He wanted to put an end to it all.

Intrusion could be a point—a specific incident or event that has the potential to interrupt our flow. For Maya (Chapter 5: Trapped), it was the point at which she came back home. It ruptured her sense of identity and her course ahead. In KD's instance, the point at which his son met with an accident seemed to have pierced his shield.

Then again, for him, this was just the last straw, the thin end of the wedge. It was an indication, the noticeable bit of much more that lay deeper within. In KD's case, several factors interfered with his sense of worth and life. The point at which he began smoking was one. It clearly left him with a deep sense of guilt. A part of him was aware that this was destructive. It intruded upon his austere upbringing, where thriftiness was a virtue and health was treasured. It was the same with alcohol, considered a funnel to the loss of many things—conscious living, stability and character. In his view, he had faltered, time and again, forsaking responsibility to instead indulge excessively. On occasion when he was awash with sobriety to confront his misgivings, or to find balance, he would abandon it, decidedly. To further mark his protest, he would promptly pursue all his addictions, with vehemence.

Intrusion could, therefore, be a plane as well, a ground of sorts, where several instances of discord or disquiet are buried as weed seeds, taking root and sprouting with time. These instances interfere with our intrinsic sense of wellness or an innate sense of rhythm—rhythm that aids our inner ability to seek an uninterrupted, expansive path through time. Unaddressed, or unprocessed, these weed-instances of disquiet grow in strength, below the surface. Then, in hot weather (a point of vulnerability or stress), they erupt, ripping apart the surface-façade of calm and control.

The surface may now be overridden with guilt and anger—from not having tried enough, not having done one's best, not exploring the heights of one's potential; guilt-anger from choosing indulgence, or helplessness in the face of perceived weakness.

Guilt-anger feeds into other forms of fear—a sense of victimhood, for instance—that terrible things are waiting to happen, from things we did or did not do, from things we gave into. Inner alarms were not heeded, and so now there will be reprisal, even damnation. An exaggerated sense of doom prevails and the slightest misfortune can take on fatal proportions. KD felt so. As did another lady in her 60s, whose trajectory into severe depression bore similar symptoms to KD's. The urinary tract infection that plagued her, she believed, was cancer, and that she was bound to die. Nothing would save her.

KD's leanings were marked with rebellion. His predisposition to developing addictions seemed actively to stem from wanting to defy something or someone, perhaps from his childhood years. His recorded statements imply his defiant stance.

Early imprints are of great relevance. Neurologists and therapists from around the world have begun to understand the power of impressions from the early years of a person's life. Research indicates that early memories are the most powerful imprints we bear, conscious or unconscious, through our lives. These are the toughest to wipe away. (Alzheimer's disease is a case in point. Those afflicted by it, first lose their most recent memories, and then have trouble with intermediary ones. Childhood memories are usually the last to go.)

Early experiences are paramount in shaping a child's approach towards love, life, work and the world. Though a child's inherent temperament plays an important role, early impressions are as significant, if not more.

The effect of these experiences may be immediate or may pan out many years later, as in the case of Nik, a young man in his early 30s.

Nik was having trouble controlling his anger. He would become violent, lashing out at the object of his anger. He had got into trouble at boarding school a few times and at university too, getting into fights, sometimes bloody ones. As a young adult, he had a string of relationships. Many of them did not last more than a few months. He didn't think much of this pattern, until he fell in love. A few months into the relationship, his girlfriend wanted to quit. She said that he had an anger problem and she couldn't handle it. He didn't believe he had a problem. It was just that he had a short fuse, he said. He convinced her to stay. A few weeks later, they had an altercation. For the second time, he struck her in the face. She left. He then sought help.

I met Nik at the screening of my film on anger. Later, we got talking. He admitted that he had an anger problem and was depressed and under prescription drugs to manage it. I asked him if he'd had a violent childhood. Had he witnessed aggression at home perhaps, between his parents? 'Yes,' he said. His father had been physically abusive, beating Nik's mother, often in the child's presence.

I asked him if his anger could be rooted in feeling helpless at the time he was a child, a mute observer watching his father pound his mother. He thought it over for several moments. 'Yes,' he said, 'I felt helpless. And when I think of it, it drives me mad.' Could the intensity of his anger be equated to the violence his father perpetrated? Yes, he thought aloud. 'I want to hit him harder than he ever could. I wish I'd torn him to bits.'

Nik's guilt-anger, too, was founded on perceived weakness—that he hadn't done anything at that time to stop what he saw, from happening. He felt weak, cowardly and spineless. That made him rage. The force of his anger was fuelled by his father's violence. He wanted to lash out harder than his father could have. In his mind, he wanted to overpower his father. His anger sprung also from an embedded sense of injustice—why had the universe allowed this to happen to his mother, to his home, to him? What was his fault, he, but a child? Like KD, he, too, bore a sense of victimhood, though his sense of being a victim had the underlying belief that there is little or no justice in the world. Injustice could happen again, anytime, anywhere. It fuelled his insecurity and fed his anger.

Childhood imprints are, therefore, immensely potent. We are most impressionable as children. The brain is absorbing all it can, just like a sponge. Experiences at that age are deeply felt and embedded. We *relive* these instances, more often than we may dispassionately recall them. Love-fear, joy-grief, trust-distrust, confidence-insecurity, and even smell, colour, taste, touch and sound—each can take on a profound association with a particular instance, and how we felt at the time.

Ria, at four, was wearing a yellow dress when her father beat her for something she can't remember. She developed an aversion to the colour that lasted into midlife, until a therapist was able to help her process it. JC was snacking on sweetened rice when his elder brother fell down the stairs. The boy got 12 stitches and recovered well. Little JC, however, couldn't bring himself to have rice pudding for years after the incident. He felt great fear, anytime it was prepared at home, or if a relative brought some over. He would feel something unfortunate was bound to happen.

Emotional associations work both ways, for positive experiences and feelings as well. A friend recalls singing a particular song in her head when her middle-school results were being announced. She had done unexpectedly well. In her mind, the song got aligned with a sense of pleasant surprise. After that instance, if she'd hear the song playing on the radio, her day would lighten up. She felt awash with confidence. While such associations may continue through our lives, the ones from childhood prove to be the most vivid, and therefore, the most influential. The mind is fresh and uncluttered during the early years and records all happenings with acute awareness.

Nik's early experiences had shaped his adulthood. The injustice he felt as a child had shattered his trust. He grew to distrust the world. It made him aloof and angry. Somewhere in his mind, it was him against the world. He felt that he was fighting most of the time. It didn't matter what or who. This attitude was playing itself out, constantly. His relationships were affected by it. His thoughts and conduct were conditioned by the insecurities he had known in his early years. While his memories of childhood were vivid in his conscious mind, the effect they generated though ran into more subliminal layers of his mind and psyche.

Childhood associations may thus imprint themselves on different layers of the mind—on the conscious mind, the subconscious or on the unconscious mind.

Imprints from the unconscious perhaps play out more potently, since they remain hidden beneath layers of the psyche that are difficult to reach and therefore unravel. The unconscious lies in the subtle realms of the mind—not as matter, perhaps, but as memory-essence. It can imbue any circuit of thought-memory-instinct in the brain, or of the senses, with what it holds at its core—love or fear, or both in some measure. (Those with talent in music, for instance, love and hear sound differently to those who are not musically inclined. The unconscious memory-essence may lend them this aptitude, infusing their latent sense of sound or rhythm with more than ordinary ability. The conscious mind may then further hone inherent talent.) The reach of the unconscious would thus be wider, deeper and more compelling, than the conscious.

Around 2005, three young women came to my studio. They had seen a film that I had made on major depression and wanted to screen it at their university. They were graduate students—two were sisters, one a friend. Among them was Tara, 21, who spoke of her affliction with bouts of mild to moderate depression starting during her adolescent years. Her sister, a couple of years older, had been her support each time. She wondered too, if depression ran in families, and what could make one member more vulnerable to it, over another.[20]

I asked her if her mother was ill when she was born. It was a question I had often thought about, after the research and production of the film. She looked at her sister. 'Yes,' she said, a moment later. 'My mother was ill. She'd had a difficult pregnancy.' 'She couldn't eat or sleep well, a lot of the time,' her sister added. 'She suffered a series of infections, probably because her immunity was low.'

This is a point to consider. When the mother is ill at the time of the birth of her child, she is irritable. Her irritability stems from her feeling incapable of dealing with another life, at this point. She's under-rested, weak and usually miserable with the symptoms of her illness, whatever they may be. Delivery, which is traumatic, in terms of pain and pressure on the body, is an additional strain. Now, there is the added responsibility of a newborn. The mother feels unprepared to handle herself, leave aside taking care of another little one who is totally dependent on her. Her irritability often stems from her own inability to do what she feels she ought to, which is to look after the needs of her infant.

The child, at this point, is absorbing everything. It takes powerful initial cues from its environment in the form of sound and touch—how it is fed, bathed, cuddled, soothed; how it is spoken to and the sounds that surround it. These determine whether the infant feels reassured or riled. Supremely sensitive in its initial weeks and months, the child soaks everything in from its immediate surroundings, like a sponge. It senses its mother's irritability and exasperation, each time it cries and is in need of comfort. It is affected by the mother's impatience. It imbibes a sense of rejection, however subtle, which settles as its first imprints.

Rejection translates into melancholia—an inherent sense of sadness. The child is almost hardwired with it. It comes to bear as a primary state, as a way of being that the child may return to, involuntarily, through different stages of his/her life, especially if the child experiences the slightest sense of rejection, in any context. She/he may not be included in a game by peers; a sibling or peer may receive preference or a compliment. An unsuccessful interview or a failed love affair later in life, all may spark melancholia. Any instance could serve to make the child reticent, like the girl whose mother was depressed (Chapter 2: The Gender Normal). She appears to have imbibed the cues of depression from her mother. She seems to withdraw, at the slightest pretext, choosing instead a state of melancholic loneliness. Her withdrawal is a rejection of people and things, in turn.

Ironically, this melancholic state may serve as a comfort mechanism for such children. It helps them expel others and retreat into a personal, private zone. This exclusion is a conscious, even hostile, expulsion, yet, they seem to draw strength from it, at least momentarily. In time, however, such negation isolates them further, and heightens their loneliness, layering an already imminent sense of rejection and melancholia with depressive load.

Another seeming effect of early rejection is an aggravated consciousness of self. Rejection leaves one stuck in self-image and in a relentless loop of thoughts: 'how does the world see me', 'how great I actually am', 'how terribly I suffer', among other such thoughts. These often underlie internal dialogue and interpretation of external events. Self-image is the central concern and is difficult to override. (Those who do become aware of the pattern of such thoughts, still require a mindful, concerted effort to break out of it.) It comes from that very rejection, which really is early humiliation. The individual is driven continually towards wanting to prove something to the world, to be of worth, to be ultimately accepted as a treasured member of community.

This self-consciousness seems more intense in the case of women than in men whose mothers may have been ill during the time of their birth. One explanation could be that men, as more valued members within patriarchal structures, receive love, care and attention from family and extended family in their growing-up years. They are made to feel special. Everything about them is subtly or overtly given precedence over their female siblings. Girls, on the other hand, may not necessarily receive the same validation. An already intrinsically low self-worth thus remains in neglect.

In any event, the mother's illness and her subsequent irritability feature as an intrusion for the infant, an early tear in its narrative of growth. The result, an innate sense of rejection at such a nascent stage, most likely perches itself on the margins of the unconscious or subconscious mind, as a code, subtly determining thought and behaviour. It could make a person awkward, restless or inhibited in expression. It could prod reactions that seem inexplicable to family and friends, as well as to the individual who experiences it. It would intrude upon a sense of inner cohesion.

An intrusion, by itself, may not be fodder enough to induce depression. Of significance is how we react to it. COVID-19-induced quarantine, for instance, has proved to be an intrusion for many. Professional and personal plans have been upset, livelihoods have been threatened and family members have been forced to live together within constrained spaces, treading on each other's toes. Many have reacted with anger and despair.

Most of us, in fact, recoil to intrusion with hurt, or rebound to it with anger. The mere threat of intrusion, slight or serious, can spark anger within us. Any threat, for that matter, is what spurs us to anger, a powerful reaction, which if unchecked, can impinge upon and inflame our inner scape more than we may imagine it to cause.

EIGHT

STUCK
In Anger

The amygdala is a cluster of neurons, the size of an almond, within the brain. It is known to be associated with our survival instincts. Whenever a threat is perceived, the amygdala sparks a red anger alert to trigger the fight-or-flight reaction. The result is fear and aggression in body and mind, to fight the threat, or to flee from it.

Apart from threat, anger is our reaction to injustice. When we apprehend injustice of any kind—from someone beating a hapless child or animal, to the stance of entire governments that we may think are wrong—we are driven to anger. It is meant to spur us to action, which is why the anger mechanism is inbuilt in us. We are hardwired with it.

While anger is our reflex to injustice, it is also a reaction to the sense of helplessness we experience in a situation that we see as unjust or unfair. Nik felt such helplessness (Chapter 7: Intrusion) as impotency in the face of injustice from the abuse he witnessed at home. Maya reacted with anger, because she felt trapped once she was back within the family fold. KD felt it in his inadequacy against his addictions and what he perceived as a loss of character from what he expected from himself. Each encountered helplessness, in his or her personal set of circumstances.

Hence, threat or injustice sparks us to anger, as does a sense of helplessness and frustration from thwarted expectation.

THE ANGER TRAJECTORY

For all its force, anger is yet a secondary emotion, driven by a primary one—fear. Fear lies behind anger. Anytime we sense the threat of violation of some kind—to our way of life or our comfort zone, our plans or expectations, our identity or our ego—we are angered. We fear a change, a threat, to how things are or how we think they should be. We fear interference with our idea of order, whatever that may be. Fear drives anger and aggression.

Apparent reasons for anger to begin its trajectory could span a spectrum, each particular to an individual and circumstance. It could start with trauma, or a sense of shock, from the unexpected. Perhaps we feel let down as loved ones don't support us, or perhaps we are circumstantially in the company of people we do not like or respect. That could feel confining or humiliating, tearing into our sense of self-worth. Someone may be threatening our sense of propriety or dignity; for instance, a colleague could be passing lewd comments or sending inappropriate pictures and messages. Or perhaps there's defiance towards our authority, by those at work or at home, by our partner or by the children. Perhaps we are defying someone's authority over us.

It could begin from circumstances or events particular to each person, but the underlying cause that stirs anger commonly is loss of control. We fear losing control—over a situation or a person, someone or something we expect to control, or to be a certain way, which no longer is so, or is threatening not to be so. That triggers anger.

This challenge to our control may be actual, or perceived. We may *think* we are losing control over a situation. We may presume it, rather than it actually happening. The more at edge we are, the quicker we will be to assume the worst and react to that assumption with anger. Real or assumed, losing control over a situation or a person drives us to anger.

Once sparked, the expression of anger takes varied forms. For some, it is a quick, violent reaction, a lashing out towards something or someone. Its onset is swift and sudden, akin to an explosion. Anyone in the vicinity bears the brunt of it, especially those who are weaker and more vulnerable. 'Very often that turns out to be the wife or the children,' says Usha Menon[21], anthropologist and professor at Drexel University, US. Or it could be employees and staff, down the hierarchical order, who are not in a position to react or retaliate.

Others implode, raging within but with little venting, outwardly. Their expression of anger is to hold it within. It could find an outlet in minor incidents, unrelated to the real cause for anger. Its expression could be oblique, through sarcasm or caustic remarks, cynicism or pessimism towards events, people and life in general.

Then again, anger may build over time, layer upon layer, growing in intensity, eventually leading to an unexpected action. As in the case of TM, who filed for divorce at 57. Married for 33 years, with two grown children, in what is considered the twilight of an Indian woman's life, TM's mother, siblings, in-laws and extended family reacted with disbelief when she told them that she wished to separate from her husband. TM had no reason to leave her reasonably affable, conventional husband, they thought. Neither did she have any experience living alone, but that didn't deter her from taking what everybody, except her children, regarded as an extreme step. She said that she felt the marriage had made her very angry over the years, dictating a set script at every stage of her life. Now with her duties done, she wished to be free from it.

Vidu's expression of anger was similar to TM's, in that it simmered before bursting forth. An engineer in a southern state of India, his life and marriage were set to follow familiar norms. He was prepared for his role as the primary jobholder and provider for his family, with the uncontested authority that comes with it. Married at 26 through a traditional arrangement to PV, a woman of his community, the couple had two children. When the children were nine and six years of age, Vidu and PV found themselves at a marriage counsellor's centre.

PV informed the counsellor that Vidu had become increasingly rude, unpleasant and resistant to everything she proposed, particularly over the past year or more. He would slap their younger son often, for trivial breaches of authority. Lately, he had begun to fling things, without warning, including the food off the table. His colleagues commented on his withdrawn and sullen temperament; at home, he was ranting all day, including at the staff at home. PV's aged mother was terrified and ridden with anxiety over such explosive, unpredictable behaviour from her son-in-law. The children were on tenterhooks, especially the little boy. PV had tried to reason with Vidu, sparring with him or beseeching him, but he'd clamp up. Unable to get through to him and with things worsening at home, her frustration drove her to consider divorce. She had visited a lawyer, but her brother convinced her to see a counsellor instead. It had taken much effort from family and close friends alike to convince Vidu to accompany her to the counsellor.

By and by, a few revealing pointers emerged. The cracks in Vidu and PV's marriage seem to have begun a few years earlier around the time their second child was born. PV suggested they move in with her widowed mother, who lived closer to her workplace. She was finding it difficult to manage their growing family as well as her responsibilities at work. She felt the move would be a more practical arrangement. It would save her time commuting, and would offer her support with the children.

Vidu reluctantly agreed. For his creed, it was very unusual for a man to live with his in-laws, in his wife's house. In most communities, this is open to ridicule, which is what he faced from his relatives and colleagues alike. Gentle jabs soon led to open derision. His colleagues would mock him frequently, attributing any passing inadequacy in his work to his altered living arrangement. Only a man with no spine would move into his wife's home, they would remind him. His relatives too would throw disappointed looks his way.

While this may have shaped his attitude early on to the arrangement, back at home, Vidu felt confined in his mother-in-law's presence. He had to watch how he interacted with his wife and children in his in-laws' presence. Instead of having the freedom he expected as a man, at the helm of all decisions, he felt pushed into accepting whatever was of import to his wife and her mother. Though they consulted him at every stage, he felt inhibited. Anything that did not have his active participation, he considered an affront. The food on the table too, was of his mother-in-law's choice. When she'd ask him his preferences, he would simply mutter a 'whatever'. He felt that he was not getting his due. Unprepared in expression to verbalize his thoughts as they came up, his anger began to build. He silently directed it at his wife. She was the cause of his discomfort; this arrangement was her idea.

TM's anger built over the years as her life had followed a set script; Vidu was enraged over time for having been denied the script he expected his life to have. In both cases, there was perceived intrusion and a blow to expectations that built anger over the years. However, their outward expression differed.

'Where the group is important, people getting on with others is important, both men and women are discouraged from experiencing and expressing anger. But there is a difference perhaps, a gender difference,' says Professor Menon[22], professor of anthropology, Drexel University. 'Men are almost encouraged to be aggressive and assertive,' Dr Andrew Samuel[23], a Jungian psychologist from the UK, adds. 'Women typically have trouble expressing anger. They've been told they shouldn't; it's not the female role, it's not the female ideal.'

TM did not express the extent of her anger through the course of her married years. The fact that women are not encouraged to be angry, plainly, in several cultures, was one reason for her anger to have simmered below the surface, instead of finding vent. Her inner dialogue was built to cajole herself out of it whenever it seemed out of bounds. However, in time, she had more clarity. She identified the cause for her anger, took stock of her resources and bid her time, as it were, to 'leave at a point when she felt no burden or regret.'

Vidu sought little clarity through his angst. He felt he had lost control over the narrative of his life and, to his mind, his wife was to blame. He held her responsible for things that had gone wrong, for this situation he was in. The more he blamed her, silently, the more his anger grew within. Even when other things wouldn't work out, however trivial, his first instinct was to blame her. It was his one point of blame, and all his force was directed to it, to her as the cause for his angst.

A DRAGON FEEDING ON ITS TAIL

The moment anger arises, so does blame. They occur together, and fuel each other. Blame someone, and anger finds a target to direct its force at. Emboldened, anger and aggression further heighten with blame to increase the inner pitch exponentially. Anger thus feeds its own ferocity, out of blame and a sense of indignation at feeling wronged. 'I am *right*!' the internal voice determines, over and over again, with growing vehemence; '*You are wrong!*'

This proves dangerous; first, because it becomes a loop of anger-blame-anger, quite like a dragon eating its own tail, locked in an intense, vicious cycle. Second, it is addictive, the feeling of anger and the sense of righteousness that comes with it. It feels good to blame someone or something. The inner scape draws power from feeling right and indignant about it. This power could otherwise be a force to spur one to constructive action, but placing blame outside of one's self, more often than not, can feel satisfying and an end in itself. Blaming another person for one's own predicament acts to abdicate responsibility for one's self to something external. 'This person, event or space is responsible for my misery' is where one's inner waters may freeze. The chances of being welded to the loop of anger-blame-anger are greater than any move forward towards a possible solution. In effect, one is stuck.

Being stuck this way for long affects the approach of the mind, the functioning of the brain and the support mechanisms of the body, as it does in depression. (Depression and anger have inextricable links.)

First, the mind scatters as it darts around at the slightest impulse, in several different directions, looking to place the blame. Blaming becomes a habit. It distracts from seeking real causes and hollows one out of clarity. The process of placing blame expends energy and consciousness. A gathered sense of self dissipates. For that too, deeper layers of the mind blame others, further. The wheel is endless.

Over time, the brain is impacted. (In the brain, an impulse or thought is translated as electric signals. A neuron thus charged with the electric signal, now passes on the charge to another neuron, forming a chain or a circuit. A pathway is created from the point of inception to where the signal may rest, finally.) When a circuit is used over and over again, its pathway becomes more defined, quite like a path in grass. The more it is used, the more clearly it forms. If one is angry and constantly stuck in blame, 'the grooves become deeper and deeper', says Dr Dougherty[24], associate professor of psychiatry at the Harvard Medical School. 'So, the emotion is aroused more frequently and easily, and the emotion may persist, for a longer period of time,' says Dr Richard Davidson,[25] professor of psychology and psychiatry, University of Wisconsin–Madison and founder director of the Center for Healthy Minds.

Further, frequent anger-blame makes one feel like a victim, by others or by circumstance, related or unrelated. Being a victim becomes a way of thought. Any strain felt, in mind or body, even a headache for instance, could be deciphered as persecution by the world at large. 'See how they work against me!' comes to be a default way of relating to anything and everything. A sense of entrapment sets in. The apprehension of being victimized spills over into the present and future imaginings. That stokes fear. Fear may become a persistent, underlying state of being. All thought may either lead to it or stem from it, or worse, both. Thoughts and emotions become wheels within wheels, within the framework of fear.

The body follows this heavy lead. Fear drives the body to stay stressed, pumped with adrenalin, cortisol and other hormones that keep it needlessly in a state of high alert. Heart rate and respiration fluctuate. Blood pressure increases. The body is tense and taut. All activity that involves nourishment, repair or growth, are pushed down the order of priority, by the brain and body. 'This is not the time to digest your food! This is not the time to heal!' is the signal the body gets, each time the stress or fear reaction is ignited. Suffused with high-strung, nervous energy, the absorption of nutrition reduces, as the gut slips into anxious, inefficient functioning. Acidity increases, particularly in cases of chronic anger-blame ignition. Discomfort from acid reflux further unsettles and irritates the body and subsequently, the mind. Vital organs and systems, particularly the nervous system, are put under enormous pressure. The immune system overworks and then, with few or no positive signals coming its way, it may turn sluggish.

With the mind darting to lay blame, the body tense and afflicted, and the brain looping in deepening pathways of fear, anger can become chronic. It would take very little provocation, or none at all, to trigger outbursts of anger disproportionate to the context it is expressed in and at. Road rage is one consequence. Unreasonable flare-ups at work or home are another.

Dee recalls the years of her early teens for her father's temper. The moment she, her siblings and their mother sensed he had arrived home, 'everyone would be walking on eggshells,' she says. It would take practically no provocation for him to 'burst with anger'.

'He would be verbally abusive at the slightest pretext. We never knew what could make him angry. Sometimes, it was the tea not being hot enough, or if one of us asked him for permission to go on a school trip, he could fly off his handle just like that!' It angers her to recall how unreasonable he was.

Yet, she remembers him from earlier years as a loving, amiable man. Could something have changed to put him under duress? 'Well, he left his job and started manufacturing towels,' Dee's mum says. 'It was new to him. There were all these permissions to get to begin a business, and many bureaucratic procedures. He found it frustrating.'

Dee's father brought his pressures home. The frustration he couldn't vent for all the obstructions he faced at work, he vented at his family. For a man who'd held a steady job for most of his life, the uncertainty of a new venture wrought his nerves. The business didn't take off the way he had expected it to. 'Those were uncertain times for us,' his wife admits. 'Sometimes we didn't know if we could get past the next month.' As he ate away into his reserves, his insecurity heightened and his fears spiked. Further, the stress of perceived failure tore into his sense of worth. It pitched his anger to a new high. Once he had broken thresholds of civil dialogue, there was little to rein him in. The more he abused verbally, the more he wanted to do it. His anger and frustration bolstered more of the same, to become chronic.

Chronic anger-blame spins loops that bear the force of *all* of one's frustrations. It isn't just the immediate event that triggers anger; it is the thwarting of much expectation, the weight of many disappointments, the blame of all injustice (perceived or real) felt so far, and the impatience and stress of all anticipation to be successful or powerful or remembered. Put together, that can form the might of chronic anger.

If Dee's father felt crushed under the weight of uncertainty and failure, he displayed no coping mechanisms. Once his anger surfaced, he expressed it without restrain. It made him abusive, ugly and unpredictable. It engulfed everything and everyone around him, causing much grief, anxiety and anger to all in close proximity. Dee's mother suffers anxiety attacks and Dee struggles with the force of the anger she feels towards her father for unreasonably subjecting her mother, her siblings and her to his indiscriminate outbursts. 'I remember, one day, he lashed out at my mother while my art tutor was at home. He called her a "bloody bitch" five times in a minute. We could hear him from across the balcony door. I think after a point, he almost took pleasure in it. It makes me so angry!'

In dealing with her dad's anger from the past, which lasted until the years when age forcibly mellowed him, Dee finds herself stuck in her own. Her reactions sometime take on the shade and expression of her father's. 'I catch myself doing and saying the things I despised him for doing. I abuse as vehemently as he did,' she admits. 'And then I blame him for it.'

WHIPPING THE SELF

Blame may not necessarily be placed on others or on external circumstance alone. Its force could be pointed towards one's own self. The propensity to place blame within, for missed opportunities or perceived failure, acutely distresses the inner balance. It is as potent in causing disequilibrium and angst as the frustration one feels in holding others responsible for things gone wrong.

Self-blame, within a reasonable context and to a measure, may serve as a tool for reflection. However, more often than not, it breaks beyond its constructive use to indiscriminately urge the power of rage within. The mind calls itself names. These can be intense expletives and violent imaginings. It degrades itself and whips itself. Most of all, it calls itself a failure. The brain rages at this professed failure, while simultaneously pushing every system to perform and counter the notion of having flopped. A sense of urgency pervades the mind and psyche. Impatience heightens.

The contradiction is immense—one part is stuck in anger-blame, another pushes desperately to move on to disprove the belief of having failed. The image is akin to having a leash around one's own neck, tightly held in one hand, while the other hand wields a whip and flogs one, in a desperate bid to move on to negate failure.

Vital energy, overwhelmed with anger-blame, is expended on the fight within. The body, injured and compromised by the effect of anger, is pushed further by this sense of urgency and impatience. The act of eating is also ridden with impatience. Such induced compulsion and despair stresses and strains the body and its systems to deplete resources and reserves. Fatigue sets in and the will to engage outwardly is repressed. The outcome, commonly, is depression.

Pico was 23 when she fell in love for the first time with a senior at work. A few years older than her, the man was well-travelled, well-spoken and attractive. His career was poised to take off and he had the attention of everyone around him. Pico was besotted and the man found that endearing. They saw each other for a while, and were talked about as a handsome couple. Then he moved on, unexpectedly, leaving her bereft.

On the rebound, she began to date a man who had pursued her, instead. He was younger and indulged by a rich father. He showered her with attention, and smothered her with presents. He took her around, and was always by her side. Vulnerable and unsure, she gave in to him.

The young man was high strung and in constant need of stimulation. Initially, the excitement and flux he sought worked for her. It distracted her from the grief she bore from before. But as his amusement took more intense forms, she began to feel exhausted. Her upbringing had been modest. Simplicity, routine and ethics were emphasized at home, all through her growing-up years. This new world was alien to her—the talk, the attire, the manner, the hours and the substances—all of it challenged her comfort and her roots. Yet, she stayed with it, for a while, in her defiance to prove herself a woman of the world. She'd felt betrayed by her naiveté in her previous relationship; this time, she was determined to break out of that image.

However, within the year, she felt emotionally conflicted and spent in energy. As she began to withdraw, her boyfriend expressed his disappointment in verbal abuse and once, in physical assault. It shocked her. He apologized quickly and profusely and professed his love for her. Confused, she let it pass. The next time, though, when he threatened to raise his hand, she found her voice and shouted him down. He cowered, and suddenly she saw him as a weak, fearful boy, spoilt and dependent on the whimsical largesse of his father. He hadn't worked a day in his life and was incapable of respecting anyone else's work or the processes that build character. She couldn't believe she had been with him for almost a year. She knew she had to leave.

Back at work, Pico expected a few months of focus to put her on track. Work was busy and she had little time to think of anything else. But as the year wore on, she felt more unsettled than before. Something within was gnawing at her. She began to snap at her parents every time she spoke with them. This was unlike her. She knew it and they noticed it. Her mother enquired if something was amiss. It's hectic at work and I'm tired, she'd reply, each time her parents expressed concern. At work, she increasingly felt disengaged, internally. A stance of reluctance seemed to engulf her. Her actions were ahead of her awareness of them. She went out with friends and partied hard, but felt no pleasure. Her spirits dipped; her fatigue grew. One morning, she awoke without the will to get out of bed. Her mother called as was customary, and instead of the usual exchange, Pico sobbed uncontrollably into the phone. She said she did not wish to do anything, any more.

The therapist Pico's parents took her to, diagnosed depression.

Counselling revealed a mound of unprocessed emotions. There was anger from her first relationship. She had been in love and had felt betrayed by her boyfriend's sudden and casual change of mind. She still grieved his absence and more, she couldn't deal with his abandoning her. It had shaken her confidence. Her inherent softness and positivity had been disregarded, and she felt she couldn't trust what life might bring her.

That mistrust congealed with her second relationship. The fact that she'd been with someone she could never have respected, affected her own sense of worth. She felt a loss of dignity, which was heightened by the thought that she'd partaken of his world. She hated herself for it. Her experience the second time, so removed from her own leanings and preferences, left her mistrusting of her own self. It was something she would've liked to change but couldn't, and it had cost her her respect, she thought. She blamed herself constantly for being so mindless about it. Her anger at herself burnt beyond what she'd known it to be. The cocktail—of anger, self-blame, hate and hurt—kept her stuck around a whirlpool of despair.

The power of anger is immense, but it asks for transformation—into resolve—for affecting change through thought or action. Blame can get in the way of transformation. Blame is the glue on which anger sticks. Dark and trolling, it can pull in all of one's attention and consume one's inner resource.

While stuck in blame, anger, with all its energy and momentum, drives us around the edge of a whirlpool—raging, but in loops and circles, to cause significant emotional volatility.

NINE

BLOCKED

I

Emotional disequilibrium and disorder, to my mind, have a common phenomenon at the root—congealed resistance.

A disabling resistance underlies depression, anger and anxiety. Each arises from resistance to intrusion in the past. Such resistance coagulates to obstruct any significant movement or flow onwards, to heighten the intensity of emotional strife and mental flux. Depression and anger then build and manifest further as disempowering resistance.

Depression *is* resistance—resistance to any other possibility apart from darkness and gloom. First, disappointment and frustration affect mood. Stuck at the point or plane of intrusion, rhythm and flow are seriously disrupted. The mind, unable to find resolution, spins in turns of anger and despair. Since all energy is focused on and consumed in these loops, one feels unprepared to deal with anything else or anything new, including the day ahead or the task at hand. Tasks resisted add onto the sense of backlog, of things piling up with every passing moment, deepening resistance to the new even more.

Depression demonstrates resistance to time, to the flow of it. Failure and pointlessness, inevitably, seem the only possible outcomes. Everything else—opportunity for change, engagement or positive movement of any kind—is refuted. Life, itself, is resisted.

This was the case with Arty, whose husband sought counselling for her, repeatedly, over several months. Arty had spent most of her life as a stickler for routine, waking up at sunrise for her walk, and to run a large, clamorous household with precision and pride. An aberration appeared when she began waking up later and later than usual. Her first meal of the day was pushed to around noon. She stopped reading the papers. 'I've lived my life and the world is no longer my concern,' she said. Then, her appetite reduced significantly. Attempts to feed her were met with increasing *resistance*. She was convinced that her intestines were blocked, and that she would die soon. Her personal hygiene deteriorated drastically. She resisted attempts to help her shower or change. Her sleep was disturbed. Initially, she complained of aches and pains all over her body; after a few months, she'd lie in bed and refuse to speak with anyone. Any attempt to make her sit or change her posture would be met with resistance. She wouldn't move her limbs. She wouldn't meet or respond to anyone. She would blink her eyes as the only sign of acknowledgement. It was a shut down. Her husband, son, daughter-in-law and grandchildren were all confounded. They lived together and couldn't tell of any apparent reason for the force of such resistance.

If Arty's mind was resisting every moment, so was her body. Her aches and pains, her fatigue and bodily non-cooperation would not necessarily have been psychosomatic.

Resistance plays out significantly at the plane of the body. It leads to fragmentation—in the confluence of thought and in the link between will-mind and body. It impedes the life-affirming dialogue between different systems of the body. Inherent positive and supportive communication breaks down to create a negative narrative, which, in turn, may impel organ systems to work more in isolation rather than in tandem.

We know that neuronal overactivity releases free radicals and energized particles as waste that is harmful to cells.[26] This waste may accumulate to hinder signals to the muscular system and to deter circulation. Crucial links may choke to cause physiological imbalances over time.

Body ache and pain are real, as channels get blocked, even inflamed. The upper back takes the initial load, often. I know of two individuals who've experienced depression and then subsequently, tingling in the arms. The fingers tend to get numb, sometimes, the entire arm. The grip weakens and one begins to drop things. The pressure on the arm muscles and nerves comes from the thoracic or the upper back, commonly. It seems that overworked nerve endings use more of their resources than what they are able to regenerate. This would impact neural messaging and its sensitivity to the transmission of signals, affecting body sensation and control. Signals would shoot with a lag or with hesitation, from all the back and forth of thought and doubt in the brain. The timing of response would also be disrupted. A musician's fingers may not have the same nimbleness, for instance, if he/she has suffered a bout of severe depression. In extreme cases of depression, the entire body seems listless. It resists responding to its own signals. The urge to urinate, even defecate, may go unheeded. It may require momentous effort to move.

The signals that do spur movement are the ones directed at self-harm. Even as Arty's responses were down to the absolute minimal, she mustered the will and energy to leave the house one day, in a desperate bid to kill herself. Her family found her in time, at a park a few hundred metres away, contemplating how to make death happen.

Thus, if resistance from mind-psyche has the power to impact the fine, holistic balance between bodily systems, to that effect, the brain may perceive distress and kick-start an immune system response. That would most likely play out as inflammation. Inflammation is blockage; blockage is resistance manifest. Any which way, resistance seems to be the fount.

Resistance could occur for reasons subtle or blatant. Noise, for instance, is a cause for great disturbance to those who are sensitive to their surroundings. It can instantly impact body and mind. Resistance forms immediately, as a default recoil mechanism. Then again, resistance could appear as a barrier, a defence mechanism, from the instinct to protect oneself from harm—actual or assumed. It could mount as opposition to situations or towards specific people, as counter to someone who may wish to force our hand, to lead us to do things we are uncomfortable with or embarrassed about. This could happen early on, during one's growing-up years.

The spectrum is wide—from abuse to things that are mild—such as being compelled to speak at a public gathering, as a simpler example. Vin, at six, was made to read the morning prayer at school once a month, in the assembly hall. His father was the head of junior school, and a couple of teachers who wished to ingratiate themselves with his father used Vin as collateral. Vin was too little to understand this dynamic, but remembers his dread each time he was placed on stage. Now, in his late 30s, he resists speaking at any gathering, personal or professional, even if it is important for him to do so.

Nat's case is similar. When she was 10, her mother enrolled her for classical Indian dance class. 'I didn't want to learn dance or perform,' Nat says. 'I wanted to buy books and read.' Nat continued with her classes for four years at her mother's insistence. 'She would remind me of how much time and money she was spending on me to attend dance class.'

Did she grow to like dance with time? 'I hardly had any aptitude for it. Other students in class would poke fun at me. I hated my mother for forcing me to live her desires and ignoring mine. She wanted me up on stage. One day, I refused to go any more. Mom threatened to ground me, but I wouldn't budge.'

From a quiet, demure child, Nat's resistance built over time to affect her expression in her adolescent years. 'I became aggressive,' she says. 'I'd shout a lot. It was the only way to get her [my mother] to listen sometimes.'

Nat's offensive, launched as a counter against her mum's doggedness on her attending dance class, played out to alter her expression, even her temperament. It wasn't as much the activity (an innocuous one here) that unsettled her, as the force her mother applied to keep her at it. Her resistance hardened towards both, a person and an activity. Traces of it linger as contempt towards the form of dance she was pushed to learn.

Contempt is ground itself, for resistance to form on.

Contempt leads us to be scornful of things and people. This is not an unusual affliction for those who are talented, exceptionally bright or overconfident amongst us. 'What do *they* know?' is typically the reaction that arises from disdain. We deride others and dismiss them as inferior. In effect, we resist any learning that could come our way were we to be open in approach instead of contemptuous. Our resistance strengthens to then seep into our attitude and into our approach for the day. We resist things that we have no reason to, such as going for a walk, or making an important phone call, or attending to an important document. We procrastinate for no real, explicable reason and look for excuses to do so. 'I have time,' the inner voice says, misleadingly. 'I'll get down to it when I'm in the mood,' is another common refrain. But contempt and the ensuing resistance it generates, keeps our mood fragmented and holds us back from moving on, simply, with what needs to be done. When we do get down to doing things, we do so with an underlying frustration from procrastinating and with more effort than what it would usually take.

Importantly, resistance also builds from our denial to accept certain facts that make us uncomfortable. It is the refusal to confront things that we are not prepared for or simply unwilling to admit. Anger and envy are examples that trigger discomfort. It harms our self-image to admit that we may be feeling angry or envious towards others. Even more uncomfortable is the fact that we may have acted out our impulses of envy or anger. The attempt is thus to circumvent such facts.

Whenever Dee (Chapter 8: Stuck) tried to get her father to acknowledge the years and incidents of his chronic anger, she'd come up against a wall. He would cut her short, shout her down, get up from the dinner table or walk out from the room, in his attempt to thwart the discussion. Far from accepting it, even confronting any of it would lead to impenetrable resistance from him.

A step further from denial, resistance could form as defiance, even later in life, from refusal to cooperate with something or someone.

My team and I encountered Heman during one of our shoots. He was aide-de-camp to a high official of the state. An officer in the armed forces, Heman was every bit counter to what we would have expected from a man of his training and position. He was inexplicably uncooperative, sullen and a block to anything that could have facilitated our work.

We faced the brunt of his bearing the first time when we went across to shoot an interview with his superior. Correspondence for the time and place of the interview had been exchanged in advance with the secretariat. When we arrived, Heman made us wait for no apparent reason. The room we had to set up in was free and available, yet he wouldn't lead us to it. He preferred to ignore our requests and sat at his desk, not particularly occupied with anything. He then left the room abruptly, without offering any assurance. I finally approached another officer, who led us to the designated room. When Heman accompanied his boss into the interview room, he was surprised to see us ready and waiting. He had hoped to frustrate our efforts, for us to have been unprepared and to seem unprofessional. This was out of reason, since we had never interacted with the man before, and therefore could not have caused him any grievance or affront.

It might have ended there, except our interaction with Heman was unexpectedly extended. His superior issued instructions for us to speak with others who could contribute to the project and told Heman to set up the interviews. We were bound to go along.

Over the next schedule, Heman initially stuck to his sullen, resistant self. We noticed his hostility was tempered only in the company of his superiors. To everybody else, he was either coolly indifferent or sour with. We were the worst in line—strangers who were vulnerable and dependent on his power and whim to cooperate. We bore the brunt of his surly self. He ignored us actively as much as he could, answered in monosyllables when he did and wouldn't share details of the plan ahead. We couldn't take informed decisions on when to break for lunch or refreshments, for instance, or what lights we would need for a particular location.

My team and I, however, maintained a cordial, open approach. (We couldn't afford to antagonize him further.) We included him in our discussions, both serious and fun, even when he seemed disinterested or downright contemptuous. Whenever I'd check the rushes, I'd show them to him as well. He watched disdainfully the first couple of times, and then curiously the next few times.

At the end of the final day's shoot, while packing up, the officer we had interviewed asked me what my background was. I studied history at college, I said, and then went on to learn filmmaking. Heman, sitting in a corner, arms crossed, legs tightly folded, all closed in, was privy to our conversation. A little later, he came up to me. 'I love history,' he said, 'I wanted to teach it.'

His admission was a revelation. Had something or someone prevented him from pursuing his preferred vocation? Would he have rather taught history than become an officer of the armed forces? Was this the explanation for his attitude, for his defiance to the coveted role he now had? That he was deeply unhappy was evident. He seemed to have decided to resist everything the work asked of him, to do perhaps just enough to keep his head above water and not get sacked. Could what he professed be the reason for his anger and ultimate resistance?

I couldn't help but think that it was.

The next morning, after I met with the superior to thank him and to apprise him of our shoot, I walked up to Heman with a suggestion. 'Perhaps you could write a history of the battalion you're part of, you know,' I offered. 'Of when it was formed, the battles it has won, the officers who've commanded it as well as interesting anecdotes.' It seemed like a plausible way ahead, to my mind, to weave together what he loved and where he was at currently.

Heman stared at me blankly for a moment. Then, for the first time since we'd met him, he smiled a little and nodded, more in acknowledgement of my offering him the idea perhaps, than in acceptance of it. It was a brief moment of letting up, but the block had been breached.

Heman and I kept in touch for the duration of the project. Though our correspondence was mostly formal, he admitted it was his father's desire to see him in uniform. While he had honoured that wish, he did so defiantly. His life had been written away, he felt. His father had been inconsiderate about his happiness; Heman, in turn, refused to let anything make him happy. He had shut himself up, in a determined, resolute way, to any possibility that could've bought joy or solace in some measure. It played out in his active non-participation in work, in life, to people or events. Every moment was one of resistance. It had become his reason to be.

II

If depression, denial and defiance are resistance, so is fear.

Fear, which underlies anger, guilt and anxiety, is resistance as well—resistance to not being in control of a situation; resistance to the possibility of a different narrative unfolding, other than what we have grown comfortable with. Fear is resistance to loss and to change. We fear that the acceptable or accepted status quo might change. We resist any shift in either our inner or outer worlds. Resistance spouts fear, and as our fear increases, so does the power of our resistance.

The ground for our fear-resistance is almost always pain. Our experience of pain, or our apprehension of it, makes us fearful and resistant. This pain may be physical or emotional in nature. It may have arisen early in childhood so that we have no conscious memory of the actual incidents that caused us pain. Or such events may well be within our conscious recollection.

Painful memories generate fear. We fear reliving them. We therefore avoid them. They remain unacknowledged or unprocessed because of our resistance to revisit them, to decode them for ourselves. That creates a blind spot in our story from experiences we wish to blank out. These blind spots and our skirting around them become a potent foundation for an array of negative thoughts and emotional streams to stem and grow on.

In CK's case, for instance, it was suspicion that took root, from his resistance to confront the cause of his angst. CK seemed driven by suspicion. A government officer looking at cases of fraud, CK's work required him to deal with dubious people, to disbelieve explanations first offered to him and to dig deeper in order to uncover any fraud that might have been committed. The nature of his work, to an extent, required him to distrust people in general.

Yet, the cause for CK's suspicious approach came from things closer to himself than any external factor. As a young man, he was given to addiction. Substance abuse over several years had nearly destroyed him, until slowly, he had worked himself out of it for the sake of his pride and his young family. He knew, however, that he had acted against his best interests and this fed his guilt. As did the fact that his actions had caused immense pain to his family. Much disquiet had been generated, causing constant unpleasant scenes at home that would haunt him and others around him.

The residue of this was that he, in fact, was suspicious of his own self. He had seen the face of his own weakness and he couldn't trust himself. Over time, this suspicion had spilled outwards, so that he found it difficult to trust anybody else as well. He believed everyone was given to the same weaknesses, in the same intensity, as he was.

CK clung to his suspicious self even because it gave him a sense of false power. He felt superior each time he regarded people with distrust. The feeling was addictive and he was prone to it. Further, he'd found reason to foster suspicion. He was convinced that it was helping him be alert and vigilant. That was misleading as well. Vigilance is an impartial, intelligent enquiry exercised with openness and fairness, with no desired result in mind. Suspicion, on the other hand, assumes the worst without basis, and then looks to find negative intent even where none exists. CK had little inkling that his suspicion was in excess.

CK's unrelenting distrust began to impact everything soft, positive and harmonious around him. His relationships had lost warmth, and his immediate family members, dominated by his presence, were dry in their approach to others, unwilling to trust and rejoice easily or deeply.

While his four children and wife were accustomed to his ways, the person who felt it acutely was his youngest son's newly wedded wife. She came from a loving, trusting family and was sensitive to the unwarranted scrutiny of her father-in-law's suspicious gaze. He seemed to question her intent at every point, which made her uncomfortable and unnecessarily self-conscious in his presence. Unable to brush this aside, both circumstantially and out of social compulsions, she became increasingly weary of this burdensome negativity sent her way. It exhausted her and made her irritable.

Clearly, the effects of CK's suspicion were destructive, for him as well as for all in his zone of influence. He showed no signs of relenting. In a way, directing his attention towards others insulated him from dissecting his inner scape. It kept him from confronting his angst-ridden recollections of personal error and guilt. He was genuinely oblivious to how deeply his personality had been impacted by his reticence to face the fears of his past.

Resistance to painful reminiscences obscures out important bits of a personal story. We evade and dodge events that have caused suffering—either to us as victims or through us as perpetrators. Denying important emotional upheavals bears out on the sequence of events in our story. It fragments the narrative and our inner scape, and complicates our understanding and accounting of the past. (This, in turn, affects our conduct in the present.) Such inner fragmentation could be extreme. The psyche may split, resisting one narrative while pushing another.

Two sides of the split may play out alternately, one after another, like the swinging of a door, from one end to the other. The sway would have the force of the resistance and push generated from the psyche. It could touch an extreme at each end—one, a resistant, holding back; the other, a frenzied mania—in thought and behaviour. It could form the substructure for bipolar depression.

Reva was pregnant with her second child when she came for counselling to Moolchand hospital. She seemed compelled to speak in an unbroken flow. Yet, there was little coherence in her speech. She jumped from one unrelated topic to another, quickly. She wanted to know everything about her profession, she said, and to be the best mother a child could ever have. She would protect her children from every sorrow. She said her family was the most loving family one could ever have, except for a few minor mistakes they had made, and that her husband and his family were extremely caring in every way possible. She had settled in very well with him and his family over the past four years. She talked about how unjust the world was and how she would always do what is fair and just. She was overflowing with ideas, inexhaustibly.

At other sessions, over the following weeks and months, she swung to another extreme, intermittently. She was quiet, uncommunicative and depressed. She felt devoid of any energy and would responding hesitatingly when she did. 'Everything is useless,' she said, 'I'm useless. Nothing good can come out of anything I do.'

Subsequently, a picture emerged. Reva seemed to have suffered emotional upheavals as a child. She was discriminated against often, and derided for being 'useless and a burden' by her mother and her two older brothers. Her self-esteem was low, and she suffered a sense of worthlessness. She had resolved to be the best in every possible way, in a bid to conceal her pain, to cloak uncomfortable happenings with a forced sense of purpose. She tried hard to circumvent any prodding into her childhood. She considered it immoral to critique her family. She felt she was essentially 'not a good person' for thinking negatively about her family, and she resisted admitting to their indiscretions even while recalling several incidents when she had felt upset and despised.

In denial of her pain, and unwilling to confront distressful emotions, Reva resisted this narrative completely. She continued to reject the enormity of hurt she had felt in the past. In her current home, Reva had had to make 'small adjustments' after marriage, she said. She did not want another child, but her husband and in-laws did not believe that she had any choice in the matter. She felt unloved and unappreciated, and lived in constant fear of upsetting her in-laws, who demanded that she attend to every chore at home, apart from working a half day's job and looking after her first born. Her husband supported his parents. Unsure of herself, she couldn't define or defend her ground. She couldn't freely express what was acceptable to her and what was not. So, she gave in completely. Her absolute compliance rendered her relationships without depth. There was no one, it seemed, she could trust or speak her mind and heart to, without fearing judgement and derision.

While this depressive burden would pull her down abysmally,

she'd push herself to an opposing, manic extreme. I'm going to be the best in everything, she would tell herself—the best employee, the best wife, the best daughter-in-law, the best mother, the best cook, the best neighbour, the best colleague, the best homemaker. She would gather all possibilities into one condensed, pointed vision that placed her at the top of life and the world. It helped to negate the crushing low of a bruised and battered image and esteem of self. Her being the best would prove to one and all (and to her own self) how worthy she was.

Her need was to be accepted and appreciated, to feel loved and comforted.

Resistance against accepting disturbing recollections leaves the root of pain and grief unaddressed. Such denial causes conflict, which may manifest as opposing inner states of thought and conduct, as a pattern for bipolar depression. One state leaves the hurt unaddressed to fester deep within. It consumes energy onto itself and renders all things worthless, including the hitherto unloved self. I am useless, I'm good for nothing, I am a burden—all such thoughts arise repeatedly. The other side of the split is anxious and frenzied. I am the best, it says, in desperate need for assurance and attention. It pushes with reckless force and with impatience to fix it all, to prove it is worth more than what others perceive it to be. There is a sense of time lost (from depression, which resists the passing of time) and a corresponding urgent need to make up for it. The mania is therefore marked by urgency. Both thought and activity are driven by such mania. The intensity and impatience of the frenzy often disregard what can be actualized and what cannot be done. In excess, it blurs the lines between desire and reality, adding to confusion and despair, when things remain unaccomplished.

Reva was able to revisit certain events in the past from where her pain arose. These incidents were within her range of recall. Therapy helped her identify them. She was able to bring them into the fold of conscious thought and address her denial of them to an extent. It took the edge off the severity of her sway.

However, to acknowledge the exact cause of pain may not always be possible. The process becomes difficult if pain has been felt very early in childhood, and one may not be conscious of the exact incidents that caused it. A drunken parent, the ugliness of violence or abuse, the loss of a loved one or a feeling of abandonment, if experienced very early on, imprint the markings of fear and grief on the psyche. A state of sadness may seep in and become inherent. It may make the individual characteristically despondent on one hand, and innately stubborn on the other. This stubbornness is resistance manifest, resistance to perceived danger and pain. Like a tortoise, pulling inward; the greater the prodding, the more stubbornly inward and immobile it remains. Because the origins of pain are difficult to trace, the obstinacy is difficult to explain and may seem unreasonable, even excessive to deal with. However, the split or conflict, here too, arises from pain-fear-resistance.

The pattern of swinging between two contrarian radical states may also trigger later in life, after an intrusion.

Failure, for instance, or what we perceive it to be, can be a cause for intrusion. To have failed at something may come as a shock to the ego, more so if success has predominantly been experienced early in life or one had expected to succeed, and is therefore unprepared or ill-equipped to deal with disappointment or loss. Failure may thus be met with disbelief. Opening up to the possibility of failure, personal or professional, causes pain and hence, the attempt to block it off.

In a bid to deny it, and from despair to disprove failure, one may be driven to a frantic state of thought and activity. Such feverish activity is usually desperate and impulse-driven (in contrast to a conscious, well-contemplated attempt to overcome one's failings). It may not be grounded enough to take actual stock of what is possible and what isn't. The probability of failure again, is therefore high, and can be a throwback into the zone of dejection-induced depression. Next, in order to lift oneself up from the depths of rising despair, the push generated may be greater; the desire to win, succeed or to prove oneself, even more fraught. And so the swing between two different, disparate streams and approaches in thought and conduct become more extreme and apparent.

The greater the resistance towards recognizing the root causes of pain and fear, the stronger the bid to block it and the greater the conflict within.

Rhythm, too, is fractured. Stop-Go-Stop-Go-Stop is how it plays itself out, akin to travelling in a car, where instead of a continual movement onwards, the brakes are jammed, ever so often. Fatigue builds. The process is exhausting. A fracture in rhythm marks mania and depression. In both phases, the mind still pushes forcefully to move ahead, in spurts.

The propensity to display bipolarity is increased if one has witnessed extremes in behaviour at home. If a parent or close relative was depressed, angry and manic alternately, the child would have heard the sounds, seen the conduct and felt the underpinnings of the sway, for it to become a latent, default way of being. The greater influencer, to my mind, is the depth of the low witnessed, since the low determines the pull and push towards mania. The child would absorb the low, especially if he/she is devoted to a suffering parent. The deeper the sadness felt for a loved one's suffering, the greater the depression and more wrought the mania. The mania may also gather intensity, since the child subconsciously feels the weight of both its own sadness and that of the parent, and thus feels responsible for pulling both his or her own self, as well as the loved one, out of the depths of despair.

Alternatively, if one parent was manic or overly dominating, and the other subsequently depressed, the child could imbibe both ways of being.

Jay's father dominated over the entire family. The man talked big, sometimes reaping imaginary results before even putting things in action. He was impatient and had a violent temper. He would invariably place trust too easily, to then be let down. The family had to bear the consequences of loss each time. All attempts by Jay's mother to make her husband see his folly, or to warn him of untrustworthy people, were met with manic resistance. He would shout her down or dismiss her advice. Her helplessness deepened over time and she became increasingly depressed.

Attached to both his parents, Jay seemed to have ingested both ends of the behavioural spectrum. At 27, under the stress of a failed opportunity, the pattern kicked in for him. The first few months saw him dejected and disheartened, uninterested in pursuing any other opportunity at work. Then, he began to talk positive in an urgent way. He listed the alternatives available to him and wished to pursue them all at once. I'm going to make it very big, he told his mother, in a bid to reassure her. I'm going to be the best. He talked quickly and vehemently, and slept little. He was impatient and unable to follow through on his expectations. Several weeks later, exhausted from the rush in his brain and body, he lost steam. Everything seemed dismal to him. He'd swung the other way. This swing was one of others that followed.

While it is natural to lift oneself up when low, bipolarity is about having unrealistic goals, way beyond what may be achievable through time, resource or physical effort. The expectations are usually grandiose during phases of mania, and are thus difficult to accomplish. Jay's father displayed symptoms of mania, sometimes bordering on delusion in his objectives. A man whose generation was raised in the 1950s and '60s, right after the partition of the country, he belonged to a time when men were probably not allowed to show any signs of perceived weakness. When angry, he would blame others, viciously. When threatened by disappointment, he would use his might to pull himself away from it. To acknowledge failure meant that *he* had failed. At no cost, was that allowed to him, he believed. Ironically, he was quick to label others as 'complete failures', instead. It was an attempt to deflect forcibly from his own failings.

Jay imbibed both, the pattern of behaviour from his father, as well as the dejection he felt for his mother's helplessness. He began to consider himself a failure. Everything was black or white. The sounds at home he'd grown up listening, especially during phases of stress, had not allowed for reasonable, detached dialogue. They had instead always been impassioned and fiery. He inherited such expression in its extremity along with the deep disappointment he naturally felt for it.

A bipolar pattern, as a split in the psyche, alternates between depression and mania. One side reveals itself after another. This could be every few weeks, every few months, perhaps every few years. The duration of time between phases though could also be as less as every few hours. A person may oscillate between two opposing states a few times a day.

Importantly, the fragmented psyche may unveil still more potently. Here is when resistance and its opposing push operate not one after another, but together, at the same time. Two conflicting states manifest almost simultaneously.

Consider the split as two hinges of a door. One remains rigid and frozen, resistant to move; the other, frantically and compulsively pushes for movement. One, inevitably, comes apart. The door is left partially unhinged, dangling precariously, without a sturdy central support.

The psyche, thus impacted, plays out in thought and deed as two vigorous, contradictory narratives.

Telly was eight when her mother died. Her father, ill-equipped and unable to devote time, left her in the care of his extended family. It was a house filled with uncles, aunts and cousins. Telly had no siblings and though her relatives were well-meaning, the girl felt daunted and isolated in this bustling home. There was speculation, too, on how and why her mother had died. She overheard the word 'suicide' a couple of times, and then her aunts would hush up as soon as they would spot the child.

Ill at ease and starved for attention, the girl began to play pranks that were beyond innocent ones. She wrung the neck of a cousin's parrot. She tore another's notebook before an examination. She mixed ditch water in the food. She poked the point of a pencil into the arm of an infant cousin. It was her way of demanding attention.

Whenever she was confronted, she would lie, to save herself from the consequences of her actions. A sympathetic aunt or two would explain to the child not to create such trouble, but the girl thrived on the initial thrill it gave her, a sense of quiet power, this ability to create trouble and command notice.

The more she lied to save herself from punishment of any kind, the more she believed her lies were true. Tired of not being able to reason with the child, the family members left her increasingly to herself. She became more alone. From deep want of a parent, she would idolize her father, who when present, would sexually abuse her.

Confused and profoundly conflicted, Telly grew into a young woman with an excessive hatred and resentment for people who were leading positive, happy lives. One part of her desperately wanted their attention; another part wanted to hurt them.

One moment she sought to endear herself to them; another moment she would trash them. Unusually bright, but coupled with a deep sense of resentment, her mind began to pull at its extremes. She would profess great interest, kindness and inclusivity, but could swing to being abusive and violent within the course of an hour. Two people seemed to dwell in her. Either one of the two could show up at an instant. For anyone in her presence, it was exhausting. As a teenager, she was unable to retain friends. Her three marriages failed. She lied compulsively, creating serious misunderstandings between family members wherever a harmonious relationship existed. She felt the urge for something dramatic to happen, and when things were peaceful, she would stir up trouble. When confronted, she displayed no concept of reasonability. In two of her marriages, she instigated legal cases against her husband and his relatives, accusing them of mistreating her. Eager to rid themselves of her and her confounding behavioural patterns, the men would pay to settle the matter and get a divorce. This became a pattern, but Telly was in denial. She was unwilling to accept her role as perpetrator. She showed no remorse for her actions, and rejected the idea that she was responsible in any way. She visualized her own reasons for her pushes and pulls, and then would believe her reasons were true, honest and justified. I'm the victim, she told herself and anyone who cared to listen.

She, too, was a victim of an abhorrent childhood. Her mother's death left her abandoned; her father left her abused.

She denied this abuse, coercing her mind instead to invent explanations both for her father's behaviour and for how it was making her feel within. Her imaginings impinged on all reality and obliterated facts. Reality, imaginings, hurt and desire became indistinguishable. She felt wronged, and she found others to blame, anyone but her father. She projected her victimization on acquaintances, or on random others within her zone of influence at any given point in time.

Her resistance to one expression of her psyche was so complete, that she couldn't see any of it. It was blocked to conscious reckoning.

Resistance, in any measure, interferes with the emotional narrative. Layered over time, it obstructs mental processes, and, when in excess, it may split the psyche. It hinders the fluid functioning of various organ systems in the body. Bodily interruptions loop back signals of distress to the brain. The immune system may answer with an inflammatory response to create blockages, and further, disruption and even disorder.

Any kind of force, to break through, is pointless; force creates more resistance as a counter. Evidently, then, the probable routes to hinge the mind and psyche to stability would lie in approaches that have the power to dissolve such resistance.

Section Three

HINGE

Madhya vikāsa chidānanda lābha

The Centre, in its expansion,
leads us to awareness and joy.

—*Pratyabhijna-shastra* (Scriptures on Recognition)

TEN

LOGIC

To pause, in moments of low, is a step ahead in hinging the mind-psyche back to its core.

Every time we feel depressed or low, we look for a cause or reason to feel all the more worse. The mind digs out experiences, impulses and assumptions that support our current emotional state. Not just the past, this state of mind is projected immediately onto the future, too. Things ahead may look bleak and forlorn as well. Within minutes, our entire life seems written away in impending gloom, despair and failure.

'It is very much a pattern,' Dr Nolen-Hoeksema, known for her work on depression and emotional disorders, had said to me in an interview. 'I characterize this pattern as a kind of snowballing effect, where thoughts may start very small—something annoying your husband did this morning. You start ruminating about that, but then the thoughts expand and grow to things that your boss or your kids did that have annoyed you. It moves to other ways in your life that you think aren't going right, and eventually you'd be thinking that everything is failing in life, nothing is going right and nothing can be done about it.'

This is overanalysis, an overkill. It is unnecessary. The mind tends to dart around, naturally. It is inclined to do so. Eastern traditions (Indian and Buddhist) have long regarded the mind as a monkey—restless, chattering, flighty and distracted. The mode of the mind is not linear.

Neither is it of the brain. A neuron in the brain handles messages from several different directions simultaneously. These messages could be conflicting ones, such as 'stop' and 'go'. One neuron may be exchanging information with an entire network of other neurons at the same time. With an estimate of around 85 billion neurons in the brain, this is a complex web of circuitry. All such activity may be taking place in a fraction of a second. Add to that various enzymes at work in the brain, that speed up chemical processes, and you have hundreds of different enzymes working on various networks of billions of communicating neurons to make brain activity intricate and colossal. Brain chatter is complex and noisy, and is further amplified in periods of doubt, angst and stress. It can be overwhelming and can worsen how one feels at such times.

It helps to know that this is how the mind and its matter, the brain, work. Therefore, in moments of confusion and melancholy, to assess our lives would, in fact, compound the low. When the mind pulls to other dark broodings, we should know that this is what it must do. Here is where we may pause. We needn't necessarily spiral downwards with it.

Once we pause in moments of low, blame is next to watch.

Grief and anger lead us to blame. Someone *has* to be responsible for our misery. However appropriate this reaction may seem, especially if the intrusion we have experienced in our lives has been violent or abusive, at this point it is of use to understand that the mind *looks* to blame. Even the slightest stumbling (as inconsequential as not finding a pen in time, or not spotting the keys in their usual place because you have them in your pocket already)—all become a cause to lay immediate, intense, and even unjustified, blame. It becomes a habit.

Raymond DiGiuseppe[27], professor of psychology, St John's University, New York, illustrates the propensity to blame.

The mind wishes to feel wronged, to find something or someone to blame for it, to hurl that hot burning coal of frustration at another.

This is a tiresome wheel. There is no end to blame. Briefly, it makes us feel good, but in effect, blame makes us weaker. It distracts us, and takes away from our ability to face or deal with whatever need be done to address the problem or task at hand.

To loosen the hold of habitual blame, it helps to realize that we have been through the cycle before, that we have *been there, done that*. The mind has spun its wheels countless times. It has identified people and situations to blame over and over again. Usually, they are the same set of people, events, circumstances or the world at large. Again and again, these spins of blame have fed anger and helplessness, and festered the wounds of the mind-psyche, to exhaust one physically and emotionally. Such internal tumult has been experienced relentlessly to the point of boredom. Been there, done that.

There has to be another way—another way to deal with the same angst, the same wounds; another way to move on.

That alternate way, as unique as it may be to each, begins to open up when we watch the blame and actually, refuse it.

One afternoon, as I arrived for a meeting and locked my car, the parking attendant strode up to me. Instead of handing me a slip, he began to holler. 'Is this the way to park?' he shouted in my face. 'Take it out and straighten it!' Startled, I looked at the car. It was parallel parked, perfectly. There was no scope to straighten it. I've been taught to park particularly well and take pride in it. I turned to the attendant to reason with him, but he continued to call me out, his voice rising with each accusation.

I felt the sharp sting of unfairness. My anger began to rise. I could feel it, from my legs, rising up my spine, like a thick, heavy, black smoke. 'I am not going to blame,' I said to myself, hoping to defuse this before it clouded my mind, 'I am *not* going to blame.' Dark, smoking anger, driving my mind forcefully to fault this man facing me, suddenly seemed unsure where to go. As I struggled to hold back, I *saw* the man's face for the first time.

He was dishevelled and unshaven. He'd evidently been standing long hours in the heat. He looked parched. It was June, peak summer in Delhi.

In that brief moment of clarity, my anger dissolved. The dense smoke within, looking to stick, given nowhere to go, dissolved into nothingness.

I did nothing for a moment. Then, speaking gently, I told him that I would be late for an appointment, and that since the car was within the slot, it shouldn't really inconvenience anyone. My tone probably broke his agitated momentum. He grumbled, but I took my slip and walked away, still struck by the dissolution of anger within.

It was an epiphany. I was grateful for it. Had I reacted to him with blame and anger, I would have carried the burning residue of it through the day, perhaps through the week. That would have thrown open older wounds of humiliation or discrimination.

Blame, fleetingly, can help identify fault. It can lead one to see what is wrong, and where. However, the mind can do that quite by itself, more lucidly and without the fury of blame. It can apply itself to detect, calmly, what didn't work and what needs intervention or course correction.

Watching our ready propensity to blame doesn't necessarily stop it from arising, no more than watching anger can prevent it from sparking. Anger-blame does spark, but being aware of it as it happens, slowly begins to strengthen the circuits that oversee and regulate the emotion in the brain.

'Strengthening those areas in the brain which are important in the regulation of emotion, facilitate a rapid return to baseline, following a provocation,' says Dr Davidson[28], psychologist and psychiatrist at Madison–Wisconsin University. The founder and director of Healthy Minds, Dr Davidson's lifelong research has focused on the brain and emotion. His lab, among other studies, has mapped the brains of those who practise long-term meditation, to see if indeed such brains reflect any specific change. 'In particular, there's activation in the prefrontal cortex, which plays a very important role in the regulation of emotion as well as attention. So it is not as if they (who practise meditation) blocked the negative emotion out. They showed a strong reaction, but they also showed a reaction which helped dissipate the emotion very quickly,' he said. Anger, therefore, does spark, but the regulatory regions in the brain that put the brakes on it, are quick to spring into action. 'Negative emotion does not linger.'

The brain's working for blame, too, would be similar. Despite vigilance, I sense blame arise, but each time the mind's *inclination* to blame becomes clear, I see its workings more plainly. It needs to stick to something or on someone, often indiscriminately, to be the glue to anger. Increasingly, I understand the pointlessness of blame, which, in turn, helps settle anger more quickly than before. I am led instead to reflect on where responsibility may lie for things that haven't turned out as expected. I ask myself if something could have been said or done differently, by others or by me, or if I'd considered an alternative. If someone hasn't delivered, did I factor that in? Was there Plan B in place? Am I angry because my expectations haven't been met? That is usually so. In which case, I try and assess the situation for how things are, rather than how I expect or believe them to be. I check and reboot those expectations, from others and from myself, and take stock of what is in my control (my effort) and what isn't (pretty much everything else).

Having done that, if Plan B fails as well, or if one is given an inflated bill because of someone else's sloppiness or carelessness, instead of flipping out, it helps to ask—*is anybody dying?*

Herschelle Gibbs apparently said that after a match in the 1999 World Cup Cricket tournament. Gibbs, one of the safest fielding hands on the South African team, dropped a catch off Steve Waugh, when the Australian captain was at 52. Waugh went on to score 120 to win the match for Australia.

At the after-match interview rounds, Gibbs was asked how terrible it was to have dropped such an important catch, to which he simply quipped—Is anyone dying?

Gibbs's retort was sharp. Sure, he'd dropped the catch; his team had lost. It was sport. No one was dead.

(Australia eventually won the World Cup.)

Gibbs faced much flak for this episode. The import of the misfield wasn't lost on him. 'Is anyone dying?' is not a loose excuse for shoddy work. Neither is it a pretext for not putting in one's best, each time. The fact that Gibbs had scored a century with the bat in the same match was proof of his dedicated effort, his ability and focus, all of which was undermined by the catch he chanced to drop.

His quip though is a useful tool. It helps take a step back and widen the lens that narrows in anger, disappointment or stress, in cutting through to what should matter, in the end.

Is the reason for getting high strung and going ballistic at another a matter of life or death?

Usually, it isn't.

Several years ago, I saw two cars collide in front of me. It wasn't a serious collision. One car had a slight dent in it and mostly the paint scratched off the bumper of the other. A lady got off the passenger seat of the second car and went charging at the first. 'How dare you?' she said, to the driver of the other car. 'Can't you see where you're going? Are you drunk?' The man sat in his seat, unmoving. I got off and walked tentatively towards him. He was an elderly man and somewhat shaken. It seemed he was trying to get his bearings. I turned to the lady. 'I wonder if he's hurt,' I said unsurely. 'Look what he's done to our *car*!' she wailed in return. I was so taken aback that I shut up. She continued to shout, and since no one was hurt, I left.

The incident stayed with me though. I grappled with the lady's reaction, with what might compel someone to act this way. As a young student, relatively inexperienced in the processes of life and their stressors, I thought that she, with her immediate concerns, had missed the bigger picture.

However, since then, I've seen myself react in the most unexpected ways when stressed, irked or upset. Those haven't been entirely gracious either. Under duress, one feels overwhelmed. The mind struggles to handle even mundane, usual stuff. A loss of perspective isn't an uncommon occurrence. There is so much of one's own to deal with, that any additional strain proves to be the final straw. One nudge, and all comes crashing down in tirades of hostility and anger.

This is why Gibbs's barb is of such consequence. *Is anyone dying* allows one to take several steps back from unnecessary aggression. It helps zoom out instantly from the taut and narrow hold of self-righteous anger and blame. It puts things on immediate hold. It prevents one from mindlessly lashing out at another that could only lead to humiliation in turn, at both ends. With a wider viewpoint established, it quickly reshuffles the order of priority to bring one back to not only what may be important, in the larger context, but also to what is important right now.

That done, the damage or loss can be assessed steadily. The loss could be in terms of time, effort or money. Typically, it is in dignity lost, and a ruffled sense of self-importance. The mind, having taken stock of the cost in whatever measure, and sobered at the very least, may now place things in perspective and address the issue at hand accordingly. It can pick up the strings and persist with what needs to be done ahead, rather than being disappointed, despondent or stuck in blame for long.

ELEVEN

BODY

Bringing excessive analysis to a stop in moments of low, and loosening the constricting hold of blame on the mind are tools to consider towards equipoise. Yet, one question remains: why *was* the parking attendant belligerent? If the car was indeed parked right, what could've made him so angry?

Leonard Berkowitz[29], an American social psychologist, best known for his work on human aggression and altruism, pointed to fundamental causes that antagonize us. 'When people are experiencing decidedly unpleasant and hot weather, they are much more inclined to be aggressive and indeed more angry,' he said. Physical pain is another cause, he added, which makes a person impatient and seemingly hostile. So much energy goes into managing pain and discomfort that little remains to deal with anything or anyone else.

And finally, two common triggers that elicit aggression, he stressed, were hunger and fatigue. When we are hungry or tired, it takes little to breach our poise.

Every parent knows this for a fact. Nothing makes an infant more irritable than if she/he is sleepy or hungry, or in physical discomfort of some sort. It helps to recall that such primary causes are significant for everyone, at all times. Unaddressed fatigue that becomes chronic can lead to chronic anger. Hunger, temporarily even, can drive us to aggression.

From that rude parking attendant who might have been sick from the heat, to a boss or colleague who might have found time for lunch closer to dusk, it helps to know that these are compelling triggers to what may seem like irrational anger, unfairly directed our way. It helps more to know that these basic states could be triggers to our own anger, and not necessarily anything more complicated.

Turning our focus to the body is an effective way to reach the mind.

We are built for activity. Our bodies are designed to move, and movement, in turn, keeps the body and brain in order. If we are physically sluggish, we aren't mentally alert either.

The brain, an organ akin to a muscle, has arteries and arterioles that bring it blood. Exercise strengthens these muscles and assists blood circulation. It is known to enhance genesis in the hippocampus, a brain structure that apparently regulates learning, emotion and memory. The brain's cognitive ability finds support in its ability to adapt, learn and grow. Physical activity keeps the brain and mind attentive.

Time spent aimlessly on gadgets and screens takes away from physical strength and endurance. Children and adolescents are most at risk since their mental and physical development can be hugely and irrevocably impacted by the addiction that comes from screens. Take a phone or a screen away from a child and he/she reacts violently, as much as an alcoholic denied alcohol, or a substance abuser denied drugs.

In 2016, the All India Institute of Medical Sciences (AIIMS) set up a special psychiatric out patient department for those addicted to social media, online gaming and other forms of cyber addiction. Teachers in schools and colleges along with parents voiced growing concern over falling grades and increased substance abuse among children and adolescents addicted to the internet. Medical experts were marking symptoms of moderate to severe behavioural and psychiatric problems among such youngsters. A particular case highlighted the conduct of two adolescent brothers in Delhi who were hooked to online gaming for 18 hours a day! They ignored thieves who broke into their house, twice, and reached a stage where they were urinating and defecating in their chairs, while playing online.[30]

In addition to excessive use of social media and compulsive online gaming, internet addiction disorder (IAD) includes net compulsions such as excessive shopping, gambling and trading as well as cyber-sexual and cyber-virtual addiction.

Indiscriminate use of the internet through mobiles and other screens takes away from cognitive tasks, which really is any activity demanding attention. Eating and drinking become mindless activities when hooked to a screen. Sleep patterns and the body's circadian rhythm are subsequently thrown into disarray when net interactions continue into early hours of the morning. Here, too, exhaustion sets in; irritability increases from lack of proper sleep; attention suffers in class or at work. Most of all, anxiety builds exponentially as the technology in use pressures us from a barrage of views and voices. Bullying and malice are rampant and often unchecked. Young minds, riding naturally on emotional intensity, are severely affected.

Additionally, the speed at which it comes is difficult to keep up with. Our ability to absorb, think and analyse is inundated by the volume of information and the unrelenting haste of it that characterize our times and milieu. 'When the brain is bombarded with instant messages, its reactions are also instant,' says Dr Sumantra Chattarji[31], at the National Centre for Biological Sciences, Bangalore. His research focuses on circuits of fear and on how emotional memories are formed. 'This means, we are increasingly using those reflexes, circuits and regions of the brain that are meant for instant *reactions*. The other parts, which are used for more reflective thought and analysis, and more sustained responses, may correspondingly be falling into disuse. We stand at risk of losing that potential.'

Being under pressure to react instantly so much of the time would make the brain more edgy and anxious. The calmer, more reflective regions of the brain would consequently be less in use. The mind would be less patient and less resilient. It would search for instant gratification and, in turn, instant stimulation, much of the time. Stimulation would have to be more and more extreme, to sustain interest. Anything less, to such a mind, would seem boring. All things quiet and still would be at risk of being dismissed. That would result in more extreme and reactive traits, in personality and behaviour.

In addition to the impact on the brain, such emphasis on speed ignores the rhythms of the body and the time that we need to process our emotions. The effect, apart from major stressors on the body, is a scattered sense of self, or a tear in the wholeness that we inherently strive for. We are crushed under the weight of all that which we cannot possibly keep up with.

Most of all, essential physical activity is compromised.

A friend voiced his concern about parenting in these days of screens. He wondered if he could instil a sense of balance for his two young children—one nine, and the other, six years old. If they can play any one sport of their choice, that would help, I suggested. I know of a 12-year-old who took to football when he was about eight. He wakes up willingly early in the morning to practise before school begins. Playing on a field as a member of a team allows him social interaction and social integration with peers in real time and space. It keeps him physically engaged and mentally alert. At the end of each practice session, he feels the flush of accomplishment. His approach to the day ahead bears a sense of purpose. By eight at night, he is so tired, that there is not much scope for screen time.

Sport also leads to a quieter brain. Nina Kraus, professor and director of the Auditory Neuroscience Laboratory at Northwestern University's Evanston campus in Illinois, and her colleagues studied around 500 male and female athletes, as well as an equal number of non-athletes at the school, to find that the athletes' brains were better able to filter out unnecessary background noise.[32] The athletes were better able to pinpoint, amplify and focus on the sounds they wanted. 'Basically, their brains are quieter,' she says. 'Fitness and regular movement of the body also change the brain.'

Besides sport, if a child is encouraged to explore one creative pursuit, then the foundation for balance is laid, as a matter of course. Learning how to play an instrument, calligraphy or any other activity that involves using the fingers and hands, hones sensory skills. It is known to strengthen synchronicity between the left and right hemispheres of the brain. Writing by hand or cursive writing apparently leads children to develop better language skills, better memory from forming the word and better coping mechanism from the time taken to write, than children who type instead. Using a keyboard leads to shallower processing of the alphabet, word and language, and therefore, less retention as well. Using our hands for fine tasks and focusing on a tactile activity have many benefits.

Such pursuits are of as much use to adults. Gardening or cooking are activities known to relax body and mind. Alternatively, one could exercise, however mild or short in duration. 'One of the most rapid consequences of getting onto a treadmill or walking around for even a few minutes, is to improve the ability of your muscles to use glucose,' says Dr Bruce McEwen[33], head of the Laboratory of Neuroendocrinology at Rockefeller University, New York. 'Exercise is an antidepressant. Regular exercise reduces insulin resistance and helps in the prevention of diabetes,' he says. 'It has beneficial effects on all the systems of the body and is one of the most important activities a person can do.'

If time is a constraint (as it often is), one can be conscious of the routine activity that we conduct in the course of the day. Bringing attention back to a physical task of any kind slows the mind to the pace of the body. It pauses the mind's meanderings and gives it something tangible to focus on. Any physical activity, done even for a minute or two, induces ease and pleasant focus. Getting up to stretch intermittently during work hours, walking from one point to another, eating mindfully or speaking deliberately, even, are ways to ease up. Doodling or writing a few words by hand bridges the distance between mind and body for that amount of time. The most basic activities can become harbingers of mind-body connect. Done in bits through the day, it relaxes the mind in spurts and builds body awareness.

'One good way to start is to concentrate on the breathing,' says Tenzin Palmo[34], a Buddhist nun and teacher, 'because we cannot breathe in the past, and we cannot breathe in the future. We can only breathe now (in the present). So, it is a very good and effective way of bringing the mind back into the body, into the present and into what it is doing now.'

Staying engaged and focused on any activity that soothes and settles the inner scape, acts upon emotional stability. 'The capacity to focus attention is a prerequisite for emotional stability,' says Dr Richard Davidson[35]. 'One of the manifestations of a distracted mind is that people show a lot of variability in how they respond. If the mind is scattered, it is possible that the person would not clearly assign value, or even more likely, would assign different value to the same things, on different occasions. So, there would not be consistency.'

The ability to focus attention reduces inconsistency or unevenness in emotions. Further still, it shows up in health parameters as well. Dr Davidson's lab at Wisconsin-Madison conducted a study in which participants were given a flu shot. Blood samples were then collected at different points in time to quantify the response to the influenza vaccine. 'It turns out that people who show a larger change in the prefrontal function (of the brain) as a consequence of meditation are ones who show a more robust response to the flu shot,' says Dr Davidson. Meditation as a skill that can be cultivated thus reflects in brain function. A calmer mind shows up as a link to better health. 'It is associated with better emotion regulation and with improvements in a biological measure which is reflective of health,' says Dr Davidson.

If hunger, inadequate sleep and lack of exercise are points to note, other physiological factors may urge emotional strife as well.

Cloudiness and confusion, for instance, are not uncommon among women around the time of menopause. The levels of estrogen fall and the receptors for the hormone in the brain take time to reconfigure. In the meanwhile, fuzziness or brain fog leads to a seemingly weaker memory. Difficulty in recalling words or names, not feeling present or with it, walking into a room and forgetting what for—all such are frequent outcomes of brain fog during menopause. If one is unaware of the physiological origin for a mental state, then blaming oneself for 'losing it' can heighten impatience and despair. In turn, anxiety and worry increase, which may push needlessly towards depression.

Similarly, a bout of infection can add to our perception of stress. Low immunity or weakness from an illness, either brief or chronic, could make everything seem like a burden. Here, too, the cause is physiological for *feeling* a certain way. A couple of drinks on an empty stomach, followed by a heavy and late meal could lead to a fitful night. The next day could loom dark and heavy simply because the body is under rested. With less inclination to face the day, the mind may spin its own story. *I hate this work, I can't do this any more, I need to get out of here, my life's miserable* are thoughts that cause restlessness and anguish, forcing the mind to reassess what might otherwise be a reasonable state of affairs. Overindulgence, as extra food or drink, or decreased intake of nutrition from pressures to look good or lose weight, put the body under undue strain. Waking up physically compromised with aches as a result of indulgence or over-abstinence, and then denying the cause from not wanting to change habits, also twist that inner dialogue. *Why is this happening? What's wrong with my body? Am I ill? Am I dying?* Feeling tired leads to impatience and exasperation, which, in turn, could plunge one emotionally and mentally downwards, drastically and needlessly.

Body awareness can, therefore, help avoid unnecessary mental and emotional anguish. Diet, exercise and sleep are often key to a more consistent frame of mind. A routine of sorts can enhance body awareness. While, for those in the throes of depression, it is difficult to commit to anything, yet, routine helps in the important step towards simplifying choices. It helps declutter.

MD, during stressful days, chooses to have one simple dish for lunch, every day, for several days without a change in menu. It rids her of unnecessary choice, and allows her to concentrate on getting the work at hand done. (Through a lot of the writing of this book, I've chosen my attire from five black trousers and five T-shirts in all. The simplicity of decision has allowed me time and mind space.)

'You are faced with a set of almost infinite choices from moment to moment, on the internet to the supermarket, as a feature of this modern high-tech world,' says Paul Rozin[36], professor of psychology at the University of Pennsylvania.

'Companies are offering too many options, and the development of such enormous variety is taking a lot of people's time that could be better spent by them on doing what they love.'

Apart from time lost, too much choice can overload an already overwhelmed mind. It can tip a stressed mind into paralysis of decision. (In major depression, it takes hours to decide what to wear or eat or do next.) 'Rather than actually working through and taking advantage of choice, people just feel overwhelmed and may do nothing at all, which itself is a bad choice,' says Colin Camerer[37], a behavioural economist at Caltech. 'We are seeing it reflect in neural activity of the brain. The prefrontal cortex and the anterior cingulate cortex are areas of executive function and reward. They help us choose from a set of complicated choices, but when presented with too many choices, all these show a *decrease* in activity.' Too many choices thus incapacitate the brain's ability to evaluate. It induces confusion and indecision.

In an interesting analysis, Dr Nolen-Hoeksema[38] considered linkages between choice and depression. 'Recent generations really do have more anxiety and depression,' she said, 'and one argument for why we see more depression these days is that particularly in the United States for example, there are no rules. Everybody is supposed to be able to do exactly what they want to do. This belief system puts a great deal of responsibility and almost an overwhelming degree of choice in people's hands that can be difficult, especially for adolescents, to deal with. This can be very hard for them to sort out sometimes.'

Routine can help alleviate anxiety. The mind frees itself from having to constantly negotiate through superficial and endless possibilities that bombard us through real or virtual interface, every moment of the day. Instead, with a simple structure carved out in chunks of time, one can pay heed to the activity broadly assigned to a particular time.

Apportioning an hour to any one activity, work or pleasure,

is good to pursue initially. For those who have an unstructured day from too much time at hand, or for those who wish to return to work after a break/sabbatical, this becomes a reference point, and is a useful way to begin.

Ash, suffering moderate depression, began to break out by walking in the park for half an hour, early evening. He would drive to a particularly large garden a few of miles away from home. While the drive took him almost as much time as the walk, it kept him engaged. He liked to drive and it provided him with reason to pull out his car and set off to an assigned spot of his choosing. Through varying energy levels and mood swings, he persisted with this activity for several weeks. Then, he began to meet a friend for coffee or would saunter in the marketplace a couple of times a week, after his walk. After a few more weeks, he committed to an hour of work a day. Initially, he'd write a couple of sentences or send out a single email and expect an immediate and hugely positive response in return. For him to focus even for a short while was an effort and he expected appreciation for it. When that would not happen, he would struggle with instant and acute dejection, of wanting to pull back or recklessly wishing to 'throw it all away'. Yet, through enough bad days to pull him back, he stuck with his walk and with a wavering work routine. An obstinate streak was useful to keep him at it. He tempered his expectations and focused on 'just getting that one thing done for the day'.

To Ash's point, experts realize that those who promise themselves too much, in major depression or in phases of elation of bipolar depression, actually make themselves more susceptible to disappointment. Since the expectation is usually high and intense, the disappointment from its non-accomplishment too is extreme. This keeps people with depression stuck in their episodic cycles.

Psychotherapists thus advise to watch the tone of self-promises and commitments. It helps to temper these down to expect less from oneself rather than more. It also helps to make a commitment for a shorter duration of time—perhaps for the week ahead at best or more realistically, for one day at a time, as Ash did. These are targets that one can meet, and if one doesn't, the ensuing disillusionment is milder and easier to deal with.

Persistence is key. A depressive episode can sear into one's confidence and take it apart. It is not uncommon for those overcoming depression to put out a little work and expect much affirmation in return. It helps if loved ones or colleagues are sensitive to this need for reassurance, and persist alongside. With each day being a struggle, it may seem like one step forward and two steps back. To persist, nonetheless, regardless of outcome, helps shed baggage, among other things.

Ash advises listing things down, such as calling a friend, looking up a reference, going for a walk, doing yoga, and on good days, meeting up with a potential client. 'When it is written down, it clears the mind. I know it is there for me to look at, and I don't need to be anxious about remembering everything or about forgetting stuff. Also, it feels real good to tick things off.'

In time, a sense of accomplishment helped strengthen Ash's coping mechanisms and his will. A year on, he started running, and a couple of years later, he ran his first half marathon. 'It was huge…such a high!' he says, beaming.

While his days are still chequered with mood swings, Ash stays with running a few miles a day, five to six times a week, and works on a flexible schedule to 'allow for bad days'. 'I try to get as much done pre-lunch, before other thoughts take over my mind. Those are the good days. On the bad ones, when I feel all shut down in my head, or when my head is spinning with depressive stuff, I forcefully sit myself down at my computer for a couple of hours, just to stay connected. I plod away, through the distraction and noise in my head. And then, in brief spells, I find focus. Those are moments when my mind is engaged. It happens in spurts but when it does, it feels good, like time well spent.'

Contrary to the belief that committing to routine binds one and impinges on one's freedom, a framework for the day, however loose, actually sets one free for those chunks of time. Routine, and the mild discipline it brings with it, is in effect a deep respect for time.

'You just have to keep at it, without worrying about results,' says Ash. 'Just doing that makes me feel less empty.'

The logical way offers tools to consider, here and now. Watching out for the mind's propensity to blame, or bringing the mind back to the pace of the breath or body through simple, mundane activity, are things to do *this* moment. They need no additional material resource to carry out, no change in place or circumstance. They can be done independent of anyone else.

Understanding that hunger and fatigue are fundamental triggers to anger and stress, for everyone, helps alleviate pointless depressive load. It tempers us from taking things too personally, when we are angry or when we are the target of someone else's unreasonable anger. Paying attention to the body is therefore important.

Simplifying choice as much as possible gradually brings one to focus on what is of import at this point in time, and picking one thing to pursue—either work or of leisure—is a good way to start the process of harnessing time and effort.[39]

These options and tools throw a spoke in the needless spins of the mind. They compel a pause, however brief, and allow space in bits, for another way to form. As mild or slight as some of these methods seem, they nonetheless support an effect that grows in ripples, on the surface of the mind-psyche. With time and persistence, layers beneath are touched. The present sparks alive in flashes—'here' becomes real; 'now' feels engaging. The possibility that a way ahead may open up, seems tangible.

Such microflow would undoubtedly engage to pull the mind away from its dark broodings. Yet, things that unsettle the emotional sphere considerably or repeatedly may be more acute, immersed within a more existential impasse. There are thus, other means in offering for deeper knots to untie, by and by. One route is through our thoughts, to reconfigure the overarching framework of our impressions.

TWELVE

THOUGHT

I

The brain and body are instruments driven by things subtler than the matter that makes them up. When we think or feel a certain way, the body and brain respond by creating electric signals and use biochemicals to process and reinforce specific thought and feeling. The reverse is true as well—chemicals in excess or deficiency cause upheavals in the body, to drive a certain feeling and thought. An exhausted neural pathway obstructs fluidity, causing lack of clarity and vigour.

Either way, a broader[40] perspective of the psyche explores the power of the subtle over the gross—mind over matter; awareness over thought. It emphasizes that while we cannot change what may have occurred in the past, our perception of it can be brought into balance, to prevent it from affecting us further. What it requires is a shift in attitude, in how we view what we experience.

One such approach, in philosophy of a metaphysical kind, urges us to recognize a fundamental principle that governs our natural and phenomenal world—bipolarity.

Bipolar corresponds to having two poles (bi = two, polar = poles), as the earth does. It also stands for two extremes or two opposites—light and dark, pleasure and pain, success and failure, and so on. Newton's Third Law of Motion—that every action has an equal and opposite reaction—states the bipolar concept in terms of forces. Every force generates an equal and opposite force. Forces, in fact, come in pairs.

Why are pairs of opposites of significance? Why may they exist and what may we understand from this pairing?

One interpretation offers that each component of a pair is real and immutable. They are opposing, irreconcilable forces and that, when confronted, we need to choose one over the other. More naturally, we are automatically drawn to one over the other. We prefer pleasure to pain, success over failure, easy over difficult, and life over death, for the most part.

A strong inclination towards one preference, without a wholesome understanding, leads us to damn the other. It pits one against the other. We regard one a friend, and the other, an enemy. With time, it reinforces two counter movements within us—attraction (to some things and people) and aversion (to others), like and dislike, want and fear. Attraction leads us to like and want. Aversion prods us to hate and fear. In effect, we are constantly in flux, between the pushes and pulls of our likes and dislikes, of what we desire and what we learn to fear.

If unchecked, the demarcation may deepen and become more extreme—the greater the attraction for one, the more forceful our aversion to the other. It is a blueprint for self-righteousness. We vehemently oppose not just one half of the pair, but anyone who we believe is allied with it. 'I am right to choose this, you are wrong to align with that.' Our self-righteousness can grow to fuel a violent disposition, even.

A second interpretation, on the other hand and importantly, is a non-dualistic one. It advocates that these pairs of opposites primarily exist not to contradict each other, but rather to give each other meaning. The light of day would mean nothing were it to remain perpetually day, 24x7x365. We would take the sun for granted and pay no attention to it, were it not to set. The cyclical, alternating darkness of night *defines* day. It lends day its value. It allows day to recur, renewed. Darkness gives meaning to light and vice versa; failure makes success sweet; pain acutely highlights the joy of all things pleasant. One half of the pair makes the other half meaningful. We value one, because the other exists and lends it worth.

Bipolarity, therefore, comprises not of two fraught adversaries. It consists of two seemingly opposing movements that *complete* a process—inhalation-exhalation, day-night, life-death, as the most obvious examples. These are natural, complementary polarities, rather than contrarian or negating ones. They appear conflicting and incompatible, but taken together, make up a mutual whole.

We see the concept of a mutual whole represented visually in the Taijitu diagram of the yin and yang, of oriental antiquity. Two interlocking spirals of dark and light denote complementary pairs. Each has a dot of the other in its sphere. The seed of one thus lies in the other. They are not mutually exclusive, but interdependent. They rest, perfectly aligned, with each other.

To understand them as two parts of a whole is considered real knowledge or wisdom of discretion. It cuts through the bias and the involuntary pull we feel for one, over the other.[41]

Further, in the Indian tradition (Hindu, Buddhist, Jain and Yogic), the concept reflects in the symbolism of the number '108'.

Considered a sacred number, 108 is a value associated with prayer and offering through most of Indian tradition. A yoga practitioner will offer 108 salutations to the sun (*Surya Namaskar*) to mark change, either in seasons or as an offering for peace. A hundred and eight beads strung together make a prayer rosary to note the repetitions or chants of prayer or mantra. Principal deities each have 108 names, assigning 108 different attributes of power, love and glory, at the least. The list goes on.

There are several interpretations of why the number '108' may be considered of import. One notion proposes that ancient Vedic mathematicians approximated the sun's diameter to be 108 times that of the earth; the distance between the sun and earth to be 108 times the diameter of the sun; the distance between the earth and the moon to be 108 times the diameter of the moon. These approximations are close to actual data.

Another significance shows up as 108 pressure points in the body, listed in Ayurveda (an ancient system of Indian medicine), as vital intersections of flesh and consciousness.

Whatever the cause, the significance of '108' lies in the symbolism of the numbers that make it up, as well as their placement.

The number '1' represents the sun, the progenitor of light, heat and thus, life, within our sphere. The sun is positioned at the pinnacle or extreme end of the spectrum of light.

The number '8' symbolizes Saturn. (In Indian cosmology, Saturn is regarded as the son of the sun.) Yet, Saturn denotes the other extreme, the brink of darkness, where no humour may mitigate the depth it touches. Bring both ends together, and they collapse into nothingness—'0', *Shunya*, the great void—potent and at rest, from which then arise the two polarities of light and dark, on either side, equally.

Thus, with 108 chants or salutations, one affirms that in knowledge of the existence of the *entire* spread, from the zenith of light to utter darkness, conceding to both and to all which lies between them, I now offer my prayer. It is an aware acknowledgement of the extremities of both poles, and everything that lies in varying stages between the two.

Through the symbolism, it suffices to know that both poles

mark our world, and that one without the other is meaningless. Both are equally important. Both deserve equal respect.

This perspective is of immense use.

If our experiences have been dark and have weighed us down, then one of the most demanding and persistent questions to arise within is—'Why me?' This existential rant takes over the mind completely. It digs into the grooves of the brain to make stubborn, relentless loops of disturbance. Neurons fire in all directions in the brain, extensively wiring up associations, people, places, sounds, odours, visuals, memories and imaginings into a large circuit of anger, blame, pain and hate. Such internal tumult can be more damaging than perhaps the abuse, violence or deprivation, itself.

Irrespective of the nature or intensity of intrusion we have experienced or continue to experience, this irksome enquiry needles us through and through—*Why? Why me? Why was I interrupted with unpleasantness?*

Here's where '108', yin and yang, or non-duality are of use. In acknowledging that the spread of life's whole consists of both light and dark and all shades between them, we subconsciously accept and resolve their occurrence. Both polarities exist, in our outer as well as inner worlds. Both will thus inevitably come to us, in one way or the other, through a person or an event or the other, at one point of time or another. Our lives are and will continue to be inescapably speckled by both, starkly and in myriad hues.

To understand and examine this view pierces through our naiveté. It cuts through our surprise and indignation for the dark and dents the resistance of our denial towards things unpleasant. It takes the sting out of *'Why me?'* If life has dealt us a blow, however obstructive or unfortunate, we view that event from a vital layer, as an unfolding of a larger course of things. We needn't freak out as much. Our bemoaning is dampened. The mind slows in its angered spin. In simply recognizing the two as a whole, we subconsciously better prepare ourselves for both, things pleasant and hostile, as and when they may occur.

Such sanction is not meant to lead to a state of anxious expectation for things harsh and severe. Neither is it reason for a fatalistic, passive acceptance of things we are uncomfortable with. In recognizing bipolarity, we are not being tutored to throw up our hands in silent surrender to things we intuitively oppose. Nor are we to inhibit our reaction to injustice. Quite the contrary! Grasping the power of this concept, first of all, allows us to unhook the hold of past unpleasantness on us. We needn't be so invested in previous happenings. Yes, they transpired and we suffered them. We may acknowledge that fact. We needn't be trapped in it.

Secondly, conceding to the existence of both opposites is rather a preparation, a firm rooting, to handle things disagreeable. They may happen, and we may be alert to their nature. The dark comes to us externally as adversity and malice, internally as a propensity towards fear, anger, sloth, arrogance, greed and envy. The light manifests as cohesion and harmony. Recognizing them, both within and externally, would allow us to act accordingly, with awareness. When they happen, we may explore how to move on from here and from now. Injustice occurs and we may transform what might have been a wild reaction to it, into stable, well-founded action.

To dissect and analyse what went wrong and why, at a practical level, allows the use of our energy for constructive, logical reflection. We need not expend all of it in getting stuck in the victimization of the 'why me' of events.

II

There is, though, a 'why' that still remains to be addressed—why the dark? Shades of the spectrum may surely speckle our lives, but why must we experience strenuous, tough patches of time, which may take us to the edge of the depressive abyss? Why may our inherent softness of heart and goodness of intent be disregarded, dismissed or abused? What purpose may that hold?

John of the Cross, in the sixteenth century, proffered that we experience sorrow and suffering for inner instruction. When pleasure and happiness make us complacent, careless or flippant, darkness brings us to depth. It realigns us with our inner selves.

Equally, much of traditional Indian metaphysical literature does not regard the dark as evil. Darkness is not only understood as a necessary precursor to light, but more importantly, it is considered the elemental stage for creation. A seed sprouts in the darkness of the earth; a child is conceived in the dark of its mother's womb.

Similarly, our path to inner strength and potential is sparked not as much in the lightness of joy, but in the face of trial, grief and even despair. It is when our path is obstructed, that we muster the strength to face and rise up to the challenge. It forces us to hone our skills and reach deep for orientation.

Dev was on an adventure trip with friends when he got dragged into the water for several minutes, surfacing once to gasp for breath. When he was rescued, he was barely conscious. A little later, revived, he sat on the deck of the boat, silent and ruminating, while his friends clamoured around him.

Never particularly driven at work, Dev was usually the first to plan the evening out, drinking with friends or just clowning around. The younger of two brothers, Dev was indulged by family and considered himself absolved of all responsibility. The 'serious stuff' was his brother's job. He took himself to be free to do as he pleased.

After this incident, something moved within him. He seemed not to have a moment to waste. He was earnest with what he was assigned to do, and alert to any opportunity to help or contribute. At home, his folks were delighted to witness such a dramatic change. His friends were surprised too. He lost some of his old hang-out buddies, but new ones popped up, eager to befriend him. No one really understood what had happened, but those who cared seemed happy for him.

Joseph Campbell, the American writer and mythologist, reiterated the concept of light and dark and the purpose of their pairing in the analogy of the Belly of the Whale.[42] Campbell submitted that a person might undergo an unexpected experience where he/she is forced out of the realm of the familiar and, as if swallowed by a whale, comes to the edge of an abyss or death. Here, the person must face the ordeals and troubles of an event or a journey that are undoubtedly distressing. The conscious personality and all that he/she is acquainted and comfortable with, is threatened or challenged. Faced with the dark, he/she must 'come to terms with its power, to then emerge to a new way of life'[43].

Campbell thus suggested that a close shave with a profoundly dark encounter serves as an opportunity to transmute our ordinary consciousness and qualities into something unexpected and extraordinary. In the face of absolute despair, one is reborn and reinvented, as the only path ahead.

Dev's experience was exactly so. He came close to death in those few minutes under water. It could have been a terrible mishap, but he emerged, unharmed. The deep impact of this incident pushed him to reconfigure his inner alignment. The transformation that he experienced seemed beyond his conscious control.

For others amongst us, who encounter anger, despair and depression less as an event and more over a period of time, such transformation can be more conscious. It requires us to recognize that the dark holds within it the seed to things of value. We can put adversity to use as a tool for inner growth.

Attributing worth to our past suffering, leads the mind to perceive the true, hidden, transformative power of darkness. It loosens the hold of fear and resistance. If both light and dark inevitably exist, and if the innate purpose of the dark and the obstructive is to lead us to greater strength or learning, then we needn't *fear* it. It will cause discomfort, indeed, or great distress. It cannot be easily mutated or wished away, and has to be dealt with, consciously and skilfully; but it reveals our inner selves to us, with piercing clarity. We see how insecure we may be within, at such times, or how vulnerable we truly are.

Coming to terms with insecurity alone is a tremendous move, ahead. That we are actually prone to fear, doubt and envy takes the blinkers off the self. The belief that we are above board is quashed. The importance or entitlement that hitherto we expected for ourselves suddenly seems inflated, even undeserving to us. Our flaws and fragility stare us in the face. The truth about us is unveiled. Time and life take on new meaning. These forced revelations brought to us by trying times and events, offer opportunity to mature and rise from here onwards. The dark, amongst other ways, is fodder for such metamorphosis. That is its work. Once we realize that, we may release ourselves from it.

The Buddhist nun and teacher, Tenzin Palmo, puts forth the analogy of a carpet, in which the deeply coloured threads of the motifs symbolize adversity. Looking at a small section of the weave, we may be overwhelmed by how much dark there is. Pulling back, however, we see the whole of it, the complete picture, the carpet as it were, and realize that the dark or black threads were essential for the whole design. There would be no pattern, whatsoever, without the threads of adversity. They bring us to beauty. A plain white, blank carpet would offer us no prospect to engage, and none to know the weave of life.

Hence, an overarching outlook that recognizes bipolarity serves as a guide to our responses to life events. It offers an approach to resolve some of our most obstinate conflicts. On a larger canvass, as philosophy in action, it better prepares us for things unexpected. It also liberates us from the stressful expectation of excessive personal control, so that when disappointment strikes, we hold back from unnecessary blame; when success approaches, our desire for exclusive credit is tempered. Knowing both poles makes us even-tempered.

We are also made more resilient and steady, not just for the bigger picture, but also in our functioning through the day. We no longer dread small obstacles. In fact, we feel almost grateful for them being small enough for us to manage. The universe isn't conspiring against us if the jar of marmalade does not open immediately, or if the car has a flat tyre. We no longer feel a rush of anger or despair. We focus on opening it, on doing what needs to be done. Instead of being part of the problem, the turn in approach allows us to become part of the solution.

Even as the externals remain unchanged, such an internal shift in attitude allows us inner space, which so far was wrought in grappling with the 'why' of the dark. We needn't struggle in questioning its existence. We can learn to watch it and move towards addressing it more efficiently, with whatever resource is available to us, at a practical, material plane.

III

Since light and dark are parts of a whole, they are, by that measure, of equal value. They differ though, in nature. It serves us to know their propensities, so that our choosing, when we do, is a conscious one.

The dark within, to my mind, bequeaths immediate power. It makes us feel strong and smug. When we are angry or contemptuous towards another, we feel an immediate sense of power. We are driven similarly when struck by greed, pride or lust. A spike in power is what we experience. Such power though, is fraudulent. It lasts momentarily. In reality, we are hollowed out from within. Even as we feel strong on the surface, the source of that strength extracts from our inner resource and resilience.

Fear and envy, too, extort from the vital in us. Fear seeps as ink does, on the fabric of our inner wellness, weakening its weave. Envy stokes the unjust in us. It makes us unfair. We wish to pull someone down, because we covet what life has offered him/her. Instead of focusing on improving our own skills and lot, we occupy ourselves with resenting and harming the other.

The dark, in whichever form it exists, therefore, *takes* from us for its power. It consumes us from within. This is why it is difficult to sustain ourselves on a negative or destructive thought or feeling for long. To dwell in it allows its power to continually consume from us. Even as it feels powerful and heightens aggression, it empties us of calm and fluidity, and makes us tense and unbending. Sooner or later, it impinges on the rhythms of mind-psyche-body.

The light, on the other hand, is its own source of power. When we are kind, empathetic or loving, we reach within to touch latent potential, which, in turn, sparks to generate its own power. It is not an exchange. It draws from nowhere and from no one. External elements may inspire us, but the light in us emerges from its own fountainhead, within. When it does, it creates effulgence as emotion and thoughtfulness and grows exponentially, like a fission reaction, reaching out to touch others in similar ways. For ourselves, we are fulfilled and nourished, from the nature of the light-act.

Light and dark therefore play out as expansion and contraction; that which bears the nature of the light will make us expansive. That which holds darkness at its core will make us contract. Love makes us expansive. Fear makes us contract. This is one way we may recognize and choose what to align with and when. Both are of use.

Dee's father (Chapter 8: Stuck) would not accept his anger and the hurt it caused to his family. His pride prevented him from acknowledging his role and responsibility in what he perpetrated on them, through his angry outbursts. He was unwilling to go over the hump of his ego. It became a wall, which enclosed him in, preventing him from growing.

For CK (Chapter 9: Blocked), however, it was pride that helped him overcome his addictions. Mired in substance abuse and a destructive routine, an ember of pride, still burning, infused him with enough desire to work on getting himself back on track, with help from experts and family. Each time he felt he couldn't do it, his vanity drove him to push forward. Stronger than his addiction was his fear that his peers might consider him a failure. That seemed more unbearable to him than the withdrawal symptoms he suffered. His pride fed his resolve. It was of use to him, until he found a jagged momentum and worked hard and persistently to smoothen it out by and by.

A dark experience or emotion may thus empower us. Our conscious response to it can help transmute its negative power to make us grow, instead. Simply being aware of its nature can help transform its influence on us.

Anger, for instance, is known for its destructive power. In one particular Buddhist tradition, anger is considered pure energy.[44] To that effect, I once witnessed a hen chase a cat, three times her size, across a sprawling compound, because it tried to get at one of her chicks. She ran after it, squawking and screaming with such ferocity, that the cat darted 50 metres and out of the gate. The energy of anger is thus sharp and concentrated. How we express it though is of importance. In moments of real threat to life or safety, revealed in its raw force, it strengthens us momentarily to push back the threat or to flee from it. At other moments, however, it asks for transformation, which is possible when we become aware of anger as it arises. Simply watching it spark, when it does, creates space *between* the emotion and its expression. In that space and instant itself, it is partially transformed. It no longer wields the same control over us. We free ourselves from its impulsive grasp and can now decide to put it to use, the way we wish to. The more and longer we watch our anger, the more aware we become of it and the greater our ability to choose how to use its energy. Significant movements—individual, social and political—have often been sparked by anger, but have sustained themselves on its transformed energy aspiring, not for violent destruction, but rather for positive change.

Anger, therefore, needn't be suppressed. It needs to be processed, instead, so that its expression takes such form for it to not feed or create more anger around. To be ruled by anger and to run our work and lives on it, is like 'running our car on bad fuel', says Jaggi Vasudev[45]. 'You make things move ahead, but the car leaves behind a terrible black smoke that impacts everyone around negatively.'

While a dark emotion can thus be of use, conversely, a pleasant experience can weaken us were we to crave for it, over and over again. Craving for things in particular enters the zone of addiction, irrespective of how wonderful the thing we hanker for is. A good thing can be taken to a fault.

Rina wanted the best for her daughter. Her desire made her obsessive and over-controlling of her only child. The girl grew to be sincere, though unsure about her own choices. Her every decision, however little, was wracked with doubt, overanalysis and guilt, from want of her mother's approval. Her mother's vociferous encouragement, on the other hand, at every step, ironically also made her overconfident. There was an inherent imbalance embedded within, which she has spent most of her life battling with.

Sumi's desire was the same as Rina's, for her only son. The boy's schedule was determined by what his mother wanted. By the age of 10, he began to lie to her, so he could wrest some space for himself. To lie then became a habit. Today, a young adult, he wears two hats—one of the person he is in front of his mother, the other what he really feels, thinks and does. Such contradiction and complication would most likely play out on his current and future relationships.

Dip went out of his way to be of help. He would spend entire days coordinating things for others in his extended family, for friends and acquaintances. He felt he was being selfless, but his support to others was costing his own business and family the attention they needed. It didn't bother him. He had a good memory and felt others would acknowledge his support and would return the favour in time. However, when the chips were down for him, he found he was pretty much alone. Most of those he had helped were busy with their own issues. They wished him well, but couldn't do what he had done for them, in return. His expectations were misplaced.

Light and dark are hence determined not only by their own nature, but also by how we respond to each, and what we do with them.

We may choose to be aggressive, consciously, if that is what seems appropriate to function with, in a moment of threat. We could be kind and helpful, if that isn't taking us away from our own work and responsibility. But, now that we are acquainted with the nature of both, we are wholly responsible for what we select and employ in our functioning, irrespective of what prods us towards one or the other. Our choice is from our free will. What we opt for bears its effect on us.

The central message of Indian philosophical thought, as I understand it, affirms this approach: My path is mine to watch. You have yours. I am responsible for the choices I make and their consequences, given any set of circumstance. You are responsible for yours, however right or wrong they may seem to me.

Henceforth, there is no space for self-righteousness, however unjust, dark or even evil another's intent may seem. Free from the shackles of judgment, I may do what is appropriate for me—to challenge, to engage or to move on. I choose out of my free will, right here, right now.

There is no one or nowhere else, to lay blame.

Everything is of use. Nothing need be feared.

A mindful way may thus serve as an umbrella, arching over the reflections of our lives. It engages our awareness and intelligence, gently. Interpreting light and dark as two parts that complete a whole, softens the impact of adversity. It primes us to accept that hardship, in some form or the other, is natural to the weave of our lives. In doing so, we are released from the trappings of overanalysis and overemphasis of previous events. The hold and distraction of the past loosens on our present. Our coping mechanisms are bolstered and we are led instead, slowly but surely, to use our energy in the present, to build from here, or just to be and catch our breath.

Yet, even as we are attentive to the nature of light and dark, and put them to use more consciously, not all may find resolution, within. The resistance in our minds, of our minds, congealed over time, are difficult to resolve by the mind alone.

For that, other means are in offering to help, which touch us deeper, still. One of them routes itself through the heart.

THIRTEEN

HEART

I

Hardship exists. It may come in any form. Accepting this fact unlocks our minds. It releases us from excessive resistance. Less resistance to tough, past occurrences helps process our hurt and angst. We can think about them more evenly and are led to consider the true, hidden intent of hardship. Adversity pulls us to depth and propels us to greater strength. It exposes us to our vulnerabilities and weaknesses. That is its work.

Such overarching philosophy of mind lends context and an approach.

It points to observe the nature of light and dark, and our responses to both. Our observation is inward and outward—in our thoughts, in our actions and in the interactions that transpire with others. That done, we grow when we put everything to use, light and dark, ease and pain, not through cold logic, but with warm reason.

For that, we have to engage the heart.

The heart, here, does not refer to the physical organ in the body.[46] It is the psychic heart, the ground and fount/source of our emotions. It imbues its essence to impact each cell. This essence leans to celebrate all that is true and just, and beautiful in both. Our bodies respond to such celebration.

Positive emotions work the same way as positive thoughts; they make us expansive. A positive sensation, as opposed to a dark one, opens up pathways in body and mind. Its energy empowers systems within us to work in tandem. It serves as a gateway to spark and integrate a warm intelligence, through layers of our being.

Such intelligence is enlivening. It remains fluid and alive to both our mental as well as emotional aptitude and leads us to openness, moment to moment. The mere act of opening up releases built-up, congealed melancholia from past intrusion and habitual resistance. This inspired expansiveness inclines to admit the things we like as well as those we dislike, to embrace more, each time we feel positive. It suggests that even if we disagree or consciously choose to align with one over another, we do so without dismissing the things we oppose.

This is why, in the concept of '108' (Chapter 12: Thought), Saturn is designated as the son of the sun, even as each is positioned at a contrarian extreme to the other. Saturn represents the dark abyss, while the sun epitomizes light. Yet, there is a relationship assigned, no less than that of father and son, to underline a connection, inexplicable at the surface but profound in its meaning. However averse they seem, we are pointed to dismiss neither. There is considerate purpose here—the dark unknowingly serves the light, as a son serves the father. The father regards his antagonistic son with patience and wisdom. One is enjoined to the other, through a bond of the heart.

Mythical stories across world traditions abound in this approach. Tales tell of blood brothers, opposed in nature—one pure, the other his antagonist. Jain mythology, for instance, speaks of Parsvanatha[47], twenty-third in the line of enlightened beings and saviours. His tale takes us through a vortex of rebirth, of him passing through many lives. Each life is a run-up to his preparation as an enlightened being, towards greater forbearance, put to test by a dark brother, who remains forever arrogant and evil. They are born in contrast, in their internal states, in intent and in deed. One is open and earnest in his seeking; the other is taut and vengeful. He practises great austerities to gain powers, all to inflict revenge on his brother. The devout and simple brother though, has to mature through lifetimes, to grow in depth, to remain unfazed by the dark and to face the event of death, each time with equanimity. His brother inadvertently helps him get there. Once enlightened, the brother of the light holds within him the power to dissolve the darkness, to absolve the opposing brother of his sins. The dark thus serves to complete the light; the light enfolds the dark.

The tale, as myth, emphasizes the bond. It points to both light and dark as useful and worthy of respect, not merely as a mental construct, but as a settling in the heart. Even as we remain alert to the nature of both in our responses, we view each from a heartfelt space. In doing so, we are freed from the grip of excessive hostility, towards one or the other.

The first stirring that diffuses our hostility and takes us towards an inclusive reasoning, is the courage to confront.

Brij was a young, gifted musician, pursuing a master's degree in Indian classical music at a private institute. An opportunity arose for a student to travel abroad and Brij was the faculty's natural choice of candidate. However, a few weeks before the date of departure, he was abruptly told that another student would now represent the institute. No explanation was offered, though there was talk of nepotism.

This was a big blow to Brij. From a family of little means,

travelling and performing abroad had meant a great deal to him. Undeniably talented, he was stung by the injustice of it all. He withdrew, sullen and pensive.

In the following years, he took up a perfunctory job to support himself, and refused all opportunities to perform music. Many offers came his way, from family functions to community and festival celebrations. He felt that they were not important enough. He was waiting for that one big break, like the one that had been denied to him. His contemporaries and colleagues, in the meanwhile, plodded away, carving a space for themselves in their art. Most were not as talented as Brij. He did not feel threatened by their progress, but his holding back fed his sense of entitlement. When I get *my* big break, everyone will know my talent, he said to himself. With each passing year, his need for acclaim grew, while he did nothing to move towards his illusory goal. He took everything to heart, focusing on the hurt and betrayal he had felt, perceiving things with a spirit of hostility. Such hostility infiltrated his bond with music. He wavered in his practice. His playing skill diminished, but he did not acknowledge or address it. Eight years on, when a younger, distant relative was offered a chance to perform at a prestigious event, Brij felt jolted out of his reverie. It dawned on him that he was standing on the fringe—isolated, lost and unknown in the music scene.

It was a rude awakening, but Brij processed it consciously. Instead of sinking further into denial, he sought a friend who was a counsellor and chose to confront reality.

'I had to understand where I really was at. I started looking at things in new light, not how they should've been or how I *thought* they were, but how they *really* were. That was difficult.' It took him many months to come to terms with his assessment, and more time to accept the veracity of it all. 'The boat had sailed, with my contemporaries on it, and I felt left behind. To accept that truth was painful. I had to deal with that fact. I'm still dealing with it.'

As he processed his past conduct, other things came to light.

'I realize I was not short on offers. Many people asked me to perform. I did not take them seriously. I didn't understand the value of each request. These were opportunities,' he admits. 'Every opportunity is a small step forward. I kept waiting for some big, life-changing event. That could not have happened, because I just sat around, instead of putting myself out there.'

Life, thus, was not to blame. Was he, then?

'I don't know what I could have done differently. Maybe I should have stood up for the injustice back in school. That played on my mind for a long time. My friends at the time told me to make a scene. But I don't like to do that. It's not natural for me to shout and fight.' Quiet and sensitive, he let things be. He chose to do so. This was his natural response, something that felt appropriate to him at the time. 'It was unfortunate what happened back then. I lost out on time and opportunity from pulling back. I see that now. It is difficult to accept, but I'm relieved too. It helps me let it go.'

Is he anxious from a need to 'catch up', or weighed by time lost?

'My contemporaries have their networks in place. They have found accompanying artists. They've travelled and performed in various festivals. They have tie-ups with different studios. Some have agents; most know the organizers of events. They are in the scene. I'm not. I have to build from now, start like a novice. People treat me like one. They keep me waiting around, and even though I'm good, they are dismissive. It's humiliating, but I don't let it get to me.' He pauses and shrugs. 'No one knows me. They have not heard my music. I sat around at one spot while everyone walked on. I've gotten up now and I'm starting to walk too. I'm focusing on that.'

Knowingly or otherwise, Brij has overridden the voice of the ego. A mind driven by the ego is constantly subjected to pushes and pulls. *How am I being perceived? How successful am I? Do others respect me enough? Is my will being done?* All such stirring, anxious and obsessive, is the voice of the ego.

Essentially designed to protect, the ego deflects attention towards others for one's own non-performance. It spins stories to hold anyone but the self accountable for failure or disappointment. Eager to take credit for success, it presumes no charge for loss or setback. In the face of perceived failure, the ego has two movements. The first is outrage, from placing blame on others. How dare they do this to *me*!

'Outrage, to my mind, is a sign of an inflamed ego,' says Dr Andrew Powell[48], psychiatrist and psychotherapist. An inflamed sense of self is easily infuriated, from a disproportionate sense of importance. Yet, is outrage useful?

'As far as justice, human rights and such things go, of course they have to be addressed, but with truth and reconciliation,' says Dr Powell. 'Outrage always stimulates violence.'

The second route of the ego, aside from anger and outrage, is to feel sorry for its self. *Poor me…poor, poor me*, says the ego, in an attempt to draw attention. *Look at what has happened to me. See how much I suffer*.

Taking cognizance of suffering is necessary, but the ego may dwell in such thought over and over again, to escape from confronting what could have been done better, or just to distract from finding the means to move on.

Thus, to be able to cut through the ego's spiel takes grit; to accept the consequences of one's own doing takes even more.

Brij chose to confront all of this. He assessed and accepted that his expectations were out of sync with his effort. To confront reality in itself was sobering. Accepting it, a joyless though empowering exercise that initially feels like a fall, face down, to the ground, helped him break out of self-delusion. He had wasted time doing nothing to actualize his desire. In effect, he had erred. *Yes, I faulted,* he told himself. *I missed opportunities in my ignorance, taking them for granted, but no more, as much as possible. If I feel my abilities deserve attention, I need to work for it.* He took responsibility for his past conduct, and mustered the courage to endure the consequences of his actions so far.

His approach proved critical at this juncture. He identified his folly, which itself brought clarity. He did so dispassionately. Had he blamed himself here, for his past errors, he could have gotten stuck once more in a rut of blame-anger-guilt, all of which heightens emotional instability. Self-blame directs anger within. It attacks one's inherent warmth and positivity and keeps one stuck in anger at one's self for perceived failure. Anger, untransformed, burns one up. Guilt is meant to flag the harm we have done to others or one's own self, but to linger in guilt dislodges the mind; it binds the mind to the past and clouds awareness of the present moment. When the mind fights to pull away, it gets thrown into the future. Here it searches, desperately, for a pleasant thought to settle on, but the shadow of guilt shrouds the future with anxiety. The mind swings like a pendulum, between past and future, obscuring the present.

Rather than dwell on guilt or blame, Brij reflected on his life and choices. He confronted his resistance and chose not to waste more time in condemning anything or anyone, including himself.

He then went a step further. He formulated a response. Taking stock of current resource within his reach, both external and inner—time and the advantage of age, money, his existing network, his talent and effort—he resolved to reinvent, to move on from where he was at, his aspirations and expectations in check, a day at a time.

'I'm angry at times and frustrated on a bad day,' he says. 'When I sit to practise, I'm not as fluent as I was. But I concentrate on what there is, on what is still alive in my music. It is enough to go with, enough to build on again. I don't know what will come out of this, but I'm going to keep at it. This is what I love most. I love music. Holding back from it made me miserable.'

Courage is a surge towards uncovering the truth, to cut through illusion. It hails from the heart. The ground of the heart, by default, looks to rejoice in truth and its beauty. This is why our natural reaction to untruth is so angered and pronounced. We innately seek truth, and when instead we come up against dishonesty, manipulation and falsehood, we are driven to rage. Yet, to see the truth, to see things the way they are, takes the surge of courage.

If the truth revealed is inconvenient or uncomfortable, courage transforms from a surge to stillness, so it may absorb the truth, however adverse. Courage is strength as well, to confront fear and to confront the dark, especially if the dark rests within, as arrogance, ignorance, malice or sloth.

Courage draws on humility, to recognize and accept one's own failings or negativity. Humility is surrender to the truth. When we acknowledge the truth and surrender to it, we go past the ego and its resistance. Its rigidity dissolves. Our functional centre shifts to draw energy from humility, from a sense of knowing one's place in the whole.

Courage is the fulcrum of humility, its centre shaft, its hinge. Together, courage and humility calm and still us, to stand steady in the face of truth; of knowing simply, at all times, that one is capable of fault, and no amount of applause or acclaim, real or imagined, may delude us from our awareness of that fact.

Once acquainted with things that are adverse within, courage and humility naturally extend outward to spot the same. If we have felt anger, fear, pride and desire, so have others. What moves within us, moves within others as well. If we are susceptible to pain and disappointment, so are others. Those who suffer habitual pain are often alert to it in others.

My mother has lived with a chronic stomach condition for many years. Unlike others who may naturally strike out in pain (as I do, impatient or sullen when in pain), her courage enables her to contain it, to restrict it to herself. When in intense discomfort, she becomes silent. If she retreats to her room, we realize that it is acute. Because she is familiar with pain, if anyone in her presence is hurting, physically or emotionally, she is usually the first to sense it and reach out. In doing so, she inadvertently puts the experience of her pain to use.

The heart is thus a mirror. What it feels for itself, it perceives in others; what others experience, it feels for itself. When clear of the dust of delusion and lament, it sees that the dark comes not just to us, but to everyone, in one form or the other. Everyone's lives are inevitably peppered by it. It may come as weakness, pain or adversity. To perceive another's weakness or vulnerability as our own, is the work of courage. *I understand why you behave this way. You are in pain/you are insecure*, says the clear voice of courage, in the face of another's negativity. *I know how that works; I've felt it within me.*

We blunt the pointedness of another's negativity by identifying with it from our own inner scape. We see the reflection of our own follies in that of others, the shadow of our own fear and desire in their intent and action. Irrespective of the specifics, we see ourselves in others, from a heartfelt space, with courage-humility.

II

Yet, there are weaknesses that we may find impossible to associate with. Some deeds—experienced, perpetrated or witnessed—are intrinsically evil. When children are abused or the vulnerable are subject to grievous violence, how may we begin to overcome the anger and grief we inherently feel? If we have been wrongly called out for things we have not committed, how may we process the indignation that shoots through us? If we are further victimized after being inappropriately accused or abused, how do we find our peace in the face of gross injustice?

Here again, courage is called upon, to see the deed as separate from the perpetrator.

Certainly, the deed is dark; the perpetrator is deluded. He/she is unable to hold back from the promise of things dark—from the immediate pleasure of power it offers. He/she is ignorant of how the dark consumes in return for its momentary power. He/she bears the consequences of his/her deeds, unknowingly or otherwise, even in the moment it is perpetrated. We realize this sombrely, sans judgment, sans enjoyment of any kind in the other's failing.

The perpetrator, further, comes from his/her truth, as we do from ours. That truth, however it is, is largely shaped by the three Es: early environment, education and experience.

Early environment impacts the human body, brain and its humanity—its psychological tendencies and constructs, its mental activity and emotional landscape. What kind of family was this person born into? Were its relationships nurturing? What were the sounds and scenes this person may have witnessed as a child? Was there love or terror, as a dominant force? Was the family able to access adequate nutrition? Did siblings compete for resource and attention? Was there parental rejection or neglect? Did a loved one die or could there be trauma from unexpected separation? Was there abuse?

We might not know specific details to such facts and a constellation of other fundamental questions. We do know though that a child's early environment and its impact are paramount in shaping its personality. Early environment may spark and strengthen the circuits of positivity, resilience and hope, and/or contrarian ones of fear and anger, which may then manifest as forceful imbalances and disorders of body, mind and behaviour. The spectrum is extensive in its permutations. Reams of research indicate, more often than not, that physically abused children display chronic hostility and aggression. A vicious cycle manifests that often leaves them perpetrating on others, in some way or another, how they themselves have felt or continue to feel—violated.

Trip was sexually abused at the age of six, by his father. 'I have to do this to you', he remembers his father saying while committing the act, 'because it was done to me.' Since then, time had stilled for Trip, with trauma. When I met him, he was in his late 20s. His mannerism resembled that of a boy—timid in his expression, and somewhat sad and withdrawn. Part of him was frozen in time in the darkness of his father's deed. The father felt compelled to perpetuate the violation he had himself experienced. Another wheel of injustice had been put into motion.

Of course, that narrative is not always dominant. A 14-year-long study on 35 families with abused children[49] who grew up with psychosocial problems, compared nine other abused children who grew up to be well-adjusted adults. The ability to learn and absorb, self-esteem, temperament and conduct, hope, as well as external support were dominant factors that worked to create resilience in those who were able to break out of the violent cycle that frequently manifests in children maltreated.

Yet, a single, overbearingly negative experience could imprint itself on a child's vulnerable and sensitive psyche to create ripples of negativity and perversion, spilling into adulthood. This fact shapes his/her truth.

Apart from early environs and the learning it compels from family and social background, opportunities for formal or informal study matter as well. What kind of instruction was this person able to access in his/her growing-up years? Was it rigid in its teachings or open to respecting differences? Was the process of education interrupted, a child yanked out of school, perhaps? Was the learning environment rigorous or callous, encouraging or intimidating? Could a teacher have messed with this person as a child in any way—venting anger and frustration on the kid instead of boosting his/her potential? Again, was there abuse, bullying or thought manipulation of any kind?

Once more, the factors are innumerable in width and intensity, as would be their consequences. This too, is part of the perpetrator's truth.

I know a young man who in his professional space finds it difficult to offer direct answers. To a straightforward question (Have you read the file?), his response is vague. He instinctively skirts the issue. It takes four questions to elicit an answer, which would be 'No, not yet.' I asked him once if his upbringing had been very strict. Yes, it was, he said, after two unclear responses and a few seconds of silence. From an erstwhile fear of punishment, this youngster is tentative even now. The fear he felt from admitting a fault in his growing-up years has shaped his expression, impacting his professional approach and I dare say, his relationships as well. By becoming conscious of it though, he's begun to catch himself at it.

One fact can thus shape patterns of behaviour and disposition.

And finally, beyond early environment and education, comes the person's experience. Were life events primarily positive or stressful? Did work prospects provide opportunities for expression of talent and potential? Was there adequate resource or a stress-ridden crunch? Were experiences of intimacy enlivening or not? Was there promise and growth or frustration from being thwarted? Did fortune favour finding support—a mentor, friends, family or community—or was she/he vulnerable and dejected in loss, in grief, in fear and in want of warmth?

Every person thus is shaped by a vastness of causes, playing off each other. The dynamism between these influences is intricate and inextricable. All of it together, constitutes his/her truth. That truth is neither greater, nor lesser than one's own authenticity. It would simply be different from anyone else's, and unique to him/her. Even twins, with the same environment, education and opportunities, would have distinct realities. Their reactions and responses, from the ground of their individual temperaments, would make each twin's trajectory inimitable.

Hence, in the face of opposition, harm or gross darkness, however slight or significant an act or event is, it takes inner courage to remind oneself of the other's veracity and the enormity of it. It takes courage, not to confront, but first to honour the other's truth, regardless of how inappropriate and different it may seem to us.

This is not to condone the act, in any way, but to separate the person from the deed. Such separation keeps us away from hatred, which blinds and binds us to destruction. Hate convolutes the chance for constructive action. Honouring the other's truth frees us from the negativity of aversion or malice. It puts the brakes on us getting pulled into the twister of another's darkness, from everyone in effect spiralling out of control.

Further, we are released from the viciousness of anger. The emotion arises, as it must, to alert us to injustice or to threat. Yet, stripped of its viciousness, it is unfettered of darkness from our end. No longer is it blind outrage. We direct our ire towards the deed and not the perpetrator. We condemn the action without damning the person. Anger remains now in its pure form, as energy to starkly evaluate and to affect change, without the desire to unnecessarily hurt or humiliate the person whose deed we oppose.

'We have to learn to say the things we are angry about in ways that are non-confrontational and non-aggressive, but still get the message across,' Susan Nolen-Hoeksema[50], former head of psychology, Yale University, had stressed. 'It is often referred to as an *assertive* response, where you tell the other person what's bothering you, but you do not make (further) accusations.'

A firm, assertive response to things we oppose grants us strength. It makes our stand clear and replaces an otherwise out-of-control, angered reaction with a move towards affirmative action.

Conceding to another's truth is meant to mitigate the knots within us that would otherwise arise from the 'why' of things—why he/she or they act the way they do; what their compulsions might be. That done, we may bring attention back to our own work and effort. It is imperative to do this, because one route to depression is when we exhaust ourselves by giving too much importance to others and their reasons, and ignore our welfare, or make our concern for the other an excuse for abdicating responsibility towards our reality. Our goodness or understanding towards the other is clearly in excess if it renders us impotent, or if our health suffers. The weight of another's truth is not meant to crush us. It is rather a tool for empowerment and inner freedom.

Perceiving the other's truth along with ours, we now do what need be done for our protection as well as that of others. Unbound by the confines of judgment and error, our actions are thus spontaneously appropriate, from the clarity of a higher reason.

A clear reason, that separates the person from the deed, enables us to keep alive the warmth of our hearts. The angst and torment from another's action, now in context to his/her truth, tempers our inclination to lash out blindly and brutally. It makes us mindful of the other's vulnerabilities and of our own as well. The context for the use of such clear reason could be momentous, as Gandhi did, or within the confines of our homes. The inner mechanism is similar.

Dee (Chapter 8: Stuck) found rest from her father's anger by placing him in his milieu, in the stressful times he encountered. 'Those were difficult times. Now that I work and have a family of my own, I face similar pressures. I imagine he felt some of the same. It brings my own tendencies into focus.' She largely feels a sense of calm since she's decided to let go. 'Everything does not have to be resolved. It's enough to accept it, I feel. I've accepted this (his unrestrained expression of anger) as part of him. It has helped me to understand him and his expression better. I've seen him with his siblings. They have to blame someone all the time and shout about it. That's just how they speak. He probably didn't know how to deal with his anger any better.'

She finds her composure challenged at times, when her father still resists any comment on his past shortcomings, or tends to abruptly cut short any oblique reference to it. 'He does not want to acknowledge it. There's no point pushing it. He's getting on, I can see that…even a little frail. I don't want to make him feel lousy. It ends up making me feel lousy. He's almost like a child now. I try not to act the way he did. I would not want to do the same to my kids…or to him.'

Dee chooses to embrace her father's compulsions. In doing so, her reactions to the past are naturally moderated. In fits and starts, it thaws excessive resistance fostered over the years. The dynamics of power, now changed, are gently wielded. She realizes how quickly she may inadvertently do to him what she has despised him doing. Placing him in his milieu—the family, the expression, the influences of his growing-up years and the times he grew up and functioned in—soothes her anguish.

KT's stance is similar. A lawyer by profession, her hours are long and unpredictable. With a husband stationed in another city, she feels pressured at the family home from her father-in-law's resentment to her priorities. She senses his disapproval. 'He doesn't say much to me, but his displeasure is evident. The expectations from a daughter-in-law remain unchanged—marriage, house and children. Little else is acceptable. It's the times our elders were brought up in, I suppose.'

With effort, she's come to recognize his insecurities, and has worked to keep her peace in the face of his hostility. 'Initially, his discouragement would throw me off completely. I'd be upset for days. I really wanted to include him in my celebrations. But he would be sullen and even angry if I was happy about something at work. It affected my confidence. I began to doubt everything I was doing. Then, I realized he doesn't have to like me. I'm not perfect...no one is. I don't have to like him, either. I respect him as a fellow human being, and that keeps me fair and considerate. I go about doing what I have to. I needn't feel guilty about that. I try not to talk with him, as much as possible. That way, my respect for him stays steady.'

Layer after layer may thus find resolve in courage-humility to face what is fact. Courage to accept both polarities, to gather them further, lies in the heart. A clear, warm reason offers release from guilt and rage. From being conscious of one's own folly, to accepting another's truth and allowing for its susceptibilities before confronting it—all take courage and a measure of humility.

The effects are powerful on the inner scape. Expectations are reset. The process of discovering the other and his/her narrative, as well as our own, is dynamic. It naturally keeps us open and ever moving within, in response. It unfastens us from a predetermined stance. Such openness generates an outlook that is expansive and earnest in its approach, and mostly unaffected by the density of another's darkness.

Blame becomes meaningless. We dissect and address the problem, whatever it is, simply, and organize to put solutions in place—systemic if required, heedful to not perpetuate the unfairness we stand to disband.

This approach is easier to adopt for impersonal things, to begin with. When the affront is personal, it may take effort to tear through the vehemence of the ego, to remind oneself of the perpetrator's truth. When this stance settles in though, it rests on the ground of the heart, poignant and empowering at once.

With the strength and clarity it offers, we may focus on our narrative and the changes we wish to effect for us to move on and ahead.

III

Onward from courage-humility, emanating from the heart is yet its most harmonizing sentiment.

Love.

I knew Sheen as a chirpy young woman in her mid-20s. She was the receptionist and in-charge of scheduling at an edit studio. Always smiling, she was patient especially when clients were peeved at the unavailability of edit suites. Sheen handled them most amiably.

Then, over a few months, she lost a significant amount of weight. She also lost her smile, appeared tired and became increasingly quiet. She began to make errors in her scheduling.

Subsequently, her interactions with clients became less genial. Her boss noticed this and told her off a few times.

Sheen was in love with a colleague, but this was problematic. She came from a provincial, middle-income family, belonging to a particular caste in northern India. Her family was opposed to her choosing anyone outside their own community as her partner. Her mother and brother felt that she would 'bring ruin to her family' by marrying so. They told her that she would have to choose between them or him.

Sheen had lost her father and was the only earning member of the family. The dilemma, of having to pick between her family and her partner, affected her visibly. Her partner loved her and told her that she was free to contribute to her family's welfare even were they to wed. He advised her to give her family more time.

Sheen's interaction with her family, though, began to deteriorate rapidly. No one would speak with her at home. If they did, it was to taunt her for creating 'all this unpleasantness in the house'. Her brother said that she was extremely selfish for wanting to marry of her choice; her mother said that she would commit suicide, if Sheen were to marry her partner. The pitch was at peak.

A wedding in the family was due, and an elder cousin, whom she loved dearly, visited one day. Sheen went up to embrace him, but he remained cold and distant. That shook her. It deepened her anxiety and angst. When the wedding date arrived, she attended it hoping to placate him on this joyous occasion, and to meet up with other relatives she'd grown up with. To her dismay, everyone ignored her at the event. Her uncles and aunts did not respond to her greeting; her cousins and their spouses were decidedly aloof. No one made an effort to come up to her.

Sheen, like Maya (Chapter 5: Trapped), found her aspirations at odds with her family's plans and expectations of her. For Maya, it was conflict within the sphere of her immediate family; Sheen experienced the pressure from her immediate and extended family, as well as her community. Each one from the community subscribed to the view that she was threatening their established order and they, therefore, had a moral right to subvert her needs and wants. For community to crush individual aspiration that may threaten its sense of order isn't always restricted to women; men too may be victims of similar pressure.

Back home after the wedding, Sheen wept so hard that her mother woke up. She told Sheen that it was her own fault for making everyone in the extended family angry and indignant, and that her desire to marry of choice was a big mistake. 'We will find you someone better,' her mother said.

This added to Sheen's woes. She was in constant fear that her family would force someone unfamiliar upon her as a suitor. Though her boyfriend said he would wait, she felt increasingly burdened each day by things that were unresolved at her end. She had been deeply attached to her father, whose love and support she missed. Her devotion to his love had given her strength to go on, to care for those he'd cared for. When he died, she had internalized her mother's grief, and had vowed to support the family in every way possible. 'I can't leave my mother!' she cried, at odds with her sincerity.

When her boyfriend had a bit of a mishap, she blamed herself for it, for putting him under pressure. Though he recovered in a few weeks, she'd begun to come apart. Now in his company too, she fell silent. She grew disinterested in work and life, anxious about how much she was to blame for all the unpleasantness around, and dejected at how things had turned out so far. She felt trapped and began to seem listless.

In desperation, her partner suggested they marry quickly. She agreed through the confusion in her mind, and they married, with 10 people in attendance. From her family, it was just herself at the occasion.

Sheen joined work several weeks after the wedding. She seemed a shade better than before, though she looked pale and worn out. Then she took leave again. She'd come down with a bout of pneumonia. She reached out to her mother, who responded, though guardedly.

Several months later, I met with her at the studio. Her smile was more willing than what it had been in a while. She seemed confident and involved in work. 'My beloved cousin reached out to me,' she said. 'He came to our home, you know, with his family. I was so happy. I wept so much when I hugged him. He wept too,' she said, 'a lot.'

A single loving gesture held such vigour that it wiped away, in a stroke, seasons of despair and distress. This young lady was disintegrating. Her cousin's visit and his reaching out proved so significant for her that it transformed her narrative with immediate effect. She felt reassured through a sense of unity, not just with family and community, but within layers of her being as well. His willingness and acceptance of things of value to her fused together the bits that were breaking within her. An inner tension dissolved, in her rejoicing his visit. Things unknotted within to become fluid.

Of course, in the period of intense familial pressure, her husband's love for her kept the ground of her being intact. His unwavering support eased and unburdened her, keeping the flow of positivity alive in bits, enough for her to bounce back so quickly. He also consciously protected her from the demands of his own extended family. Sensing her physical fatigue from continuous emotional stress, his love was keeper for her well-being. Ever vigilant to her hurt, it granted him more energy, even as he gave willingly and increasingly to her care.

The power of a positive emotion lies in its ability to grow, and to embrace the contentious, in its ever-growing expanse. For the person in whom it flows and for those touched by it, it unites layers within. Feel and focus fuse within, riding on each other with an ease that brings all together—mind, brain, bodily systems and intent, like a musician who is one with the instrument and the music. Focused ease from a positive emotion pierces through stubborn knots of congealed resistance accumulated over time. The heart's warm intelligence smelts impediments to cast a new moult, a fluid renewed, every conscious moment. Riding on such flow, our struggle stops, because we stop struggling. Love liberates, both the host and its recipient.

A child understands the value of love from the start, in whether it was received or withheld by caregivers. When love is abundant, the child feels fulfilled and can move on to exploring his or her potential. In moments of crisis or despair, such a child remains resilient. 'A loving parent will show the child ways to contain the experience of anger and disappointment,' says Dr Powell[51], author and Founding Chair of the Spirituality and Psychiatry Special Interest Group of the Royal College of Psychiatry, London. 'If the child is soothed by a loving parent, it will learn to soothe itself.'

But if in want of love, the child's temperament develops to demand attention. 'Where the environment is not supportive, not loving, the child may grow up with very poor impulse, and would not be able to assimilate, understand and digest the (negative) experience. Here, it leads to what we call acting out, an involuntary discharge which can be violent and abusive behaviour.'

Such inner violence propagates wheels of anger-blame-pain, the root of which often lies in neglect or rejection at some stage in life.

'People who are chronically angry are nursing a grievance,' says Dr Powell. 'They have some deep-seated sense of injustice... the core of that sense of grievance is—*why wasn't I loved*?'

The heart of things dark therefore rests in the light, a little black spot in the white sphere of the yin and yang. It emphasizes the inherent bridge between darkness and light, hate and love. All things dark are in want of love. Rage, resentment, violence and malice arise from the ego's powerful desire for validation and attention. Deeper within, there is hunger for acceptance and appreciation. Frustration and grief arises from this persistent query—*why wasn't I loved*? Why was my inherent purity of intent, my innocence, disregarded?

Those amongst us who recognize this fact in our own story, draw on courage to move on from it, and not give in to the self-absorbing cry of the ego. We may feel the ego's plaintive, wistful pang, but may put it to use in being sensitive towards the origins of another's pain.

Thus, love, the epitome of the heart's power, extends our ability to listen and to respond. If for whatever reason we haven't received it, we can experience it in offering it, from the fount of a stable, central core.

FOURTEEN

CENTRE

Svāsthya is the Indian word for health and wellness. It denotes soundness of body and mind, as also, contentment and tranquillity. Two roots make up the word *Svāsthya*. *Sva* stands for 'one's own', and 'natural or inherent'. The second root, *Stha,* means to establish, to stay or abide in. It is also the word for being centred.

Health and wellness, therefore, is attained and maintained when one is centred within, or established within a centre, when one is *sva-stha.*

The centre is not an actual, physiological space. Neither is it an unreal, ethereal imagining. It is rather a psychological space or point, within which we admit the impressions of mind, emotion, body and instinct, equally. Nothing is denied—our accomplishments, embarrassments, awkwardness, strengths-vulnerabilities, aspirations; our anger, concerns, hope and despair; our memories and instincts of pain, joy, pleasure, humiliation, gratification and everything else that is still alive and exerting pressure within.

There is nothing to be done, except to recognize that these forces exist in the inner scape of the mind-heart-psyche. If we practise pretence, for instance, because we dislike someone but are not willing to show it, we admit all—our dislike, our pretence as well as the reason for our pretence. They are all true. Contrary emotions, conflicting thoughts, or a tug between the sheaths—all is noted. The more the contradiction, the greater the opposing pulls and the easier it is to identify these strains and concede to them, plainly.

Even as they seem conflicting and extreme, we bring them together. Each layer has its wisdom; each pull indicates something of import. They are not all light and positive, as we might like to believe. Neither are they all dark. They are in fact, a blend of both. Both prevail, in varying intensities, firing our thoughts and actions. By recognizing both, the unpleasant and pleasant with courage and humility, we gather them and their energies, collectively. As we do, they come together within one internal space. Allowing them space leads them to settle at their worth.

It doesn't matter which seems more, the agreeable or the distasteful, the encouraging or the humbling. If dejection or disappointment seems to take more space, it is because we *expect* more positivity. An emotion seems negative and depressing because it is accompanied by an *expectation* for positivity. Our frustration is intense because of our desperation for control and change. Thus, inherent within each is another, pulling or pushing it. We bring both the dejection and its hidden strain of expectation, frustration and the desperation fuelling it, together. They are of equal importance. We take ownership of every movement that prods us, irrespective of who the mind may like to blame for it. These stirrings are within us, and they are ours, alone. Outer circumstance is merely fodder. As we own these inner spurs, each collapses by default into the centre, like the spokes of a wheel converging at the hub. By admitting to the truth of all, the centre comes to be.

Here, at the centre, amongst this flux—a mass of traits, experience and impressions—our limited and superficial identity begins to dissolve. We watch this identity, by and by, merge into one soup from all our varied and divergent inner movements. Nothing is repressed or ignored. All is sensed individually and then again, together, consciously—the child is us, complaining and wanting attention; the youngster wanting to prove a point; the adult who is mature in responsibility and loss; the anger we feel at loved ones, and our love for them, the positive and the obscure.

We re-collect and re-absorb, to rebuild.

What rebuilds from here is 'I-consciousness'—a sense of a cohesive self, an assembled and composed identity. Sanskrit records a term for it, *Aham-Bhutva*, 'becoming I.'

The 'I' here is not to do with our identity of name, material possessions and accomplishments. It differs from the 'I, me and mine' of the Ego.[52] It is not what and who we *think* we are. Instead, it emerges from an admission of our traits and desires, of imperfections and biased thought patterns. It is a confluence of our drives and experience so far, with an eye on current strengths and weaknesses. There is no element of self-congratulations here. Neither is this an act in harshness or self-flogging. It is simply an imprint from the easy and uneasy truth of all that we've known, experienced, perpetrated and felt, deeply. The seed essence of it is our ability to integrate the truth of all what we've acknowledged so far (knowing yet that all is dynamic and will continue to change and evolve). The 'I' here is our ability to rest in that truth, and to extend from it.

From here, awareness is fresh and awakened. Each time there is a stir, its counter arises as well. If we are enthused about a particular aspiration, our past failings caution our approach, to root and empower us. If we are dejected and depressed, our conscious awareness for things that have worked out, temper our gloom and impatience. If there is one, there is the other. We know it, we see it, we admit it. When all seems deathly even, we know that we are yet alive. Whatever extreme thought or emotion we encounter, there is another to counter it. We draw into the blend of all, so that a wider, realistic and effective sense of self emerges, as an internal weave.

This sense of self melds further. We emerge from the centre, which is a point of integration, where all truth, even that of the extremes, has found equal space. There is a reset. It is as if we stand at the nucleus of a circle. When rooted here, all things receive equal attention and equal emphasis—quite like concentric ripples from the nodal point on the surface of a lake, or like spokes emerging out of the hub. This zone is consciously oblivious to duality. It has admitted all, equally. Everything has collapsed into it; everything expands from it. Expansion and contraction, stimulation and rest—all fall on even ground. All has been included. All happen simultaneously. The fight for space, the conflict of one over the other, rests. There is no pressing preference pulling to a particular direction over all else. It is a point of equilibrium, from its power to be all-inclusive.

Thus from the internal alignment of the centre, we are established in (*Stha*) an inherent state (*Sva*) of equilibrium.

Here, from being at the nucleus, irrespective of what comes to us, our response is steady. Favour and ill favour, appreciation and critique, crests and troughs, dark and light find their way to us, but from the centre, all is of value. Their nature may differ, but from where we are at, all is true. All is crucial to the whole. All merits respect.

Such respect is what shows us out of the darkest abyss. Because in depression, in anger and rage, in pain and frustration, we *trash* everything; everything seems pointless, everything seems meaningless. Nothing is good enough. Our helplessness, our contempt, our dejection comes from trashing, from disrespecting and disregarding, mindlessly. We trash people, we trash our circumstance, we trash our strengths, our truth, our very ability to think, to feel, to effect change, inner or outer, in this moment. We trash the spark of life running through us, the breath as its source. We trash it even as it is the fount of energy for our trashing. We trash time—the past, our chance at the future and the present. So absorbed and overwhelmed are we with all such trashing, we forget to take a cue from what the present moment asks of us, here, now.

It asks that we observe it, and if possible, respect it.

Observing the present, gives it a chance. Respecting it, gives *us* a chance. As we observe the present, it unfolds its potential. As we respect it, we unfold ours. Without effort, we present our best to it. Nothing is too insignificant—we may be making tea, turning a doorknob or doing a task we feel will get us no reward. Every instance of offering respect does its work. In that fleeting instant of regard, our ability is engaged, our inners still. We are released of angst, which is our own energy, turned against us. Depression is the power of our survival instinct turned against us. Our force within shreds us apart. But respect for the moment leads us outward, away from the anguish, even when the present moment itself may inflict anguish and torment on us. Respect condenses our energy and our focus to take on what may come our way. It keeps us open and alert.

Respecting all does not amount to surrendering our discretion. The space where all are equal is not a dull, complacent or thoughtless zone of complete, unmindful surrender. It is not that we don't tell people back, to halt them if we are in harm's way. Here, from the centre, our repose is conscious and alert. Aggression to counter injustice and to defend ourselves still arises, but it comes from centred strength. It arises, appropriately, does its work and falls off. One is aware of its nature and consequences. There is no glorifying it. We know that the dark takes from us for its power. We put it to use with utmost discretion, only if there is no other alternative. Beyond the moment, though, our responses abide neither in negative nor in positive. While there is no obligation to dwell in pride, ego or anger, neither do we immerse ourselves in self-righteous goodness. That corrupts equally. The positive as the expansive is experienced joyfully, responsibly and gratefully. That too serves its purpose and drifts away. Pushed beyond its purpose, the positive's expansiveness scatters. To continuously revisit and relive a moment of appreciation or accomplishment in our mind's eye, just to feel good, stokes our pride and ego. The light therefore scatters too thin and leads instead to darkness. We are alert to that. No compulsion exists to cling to any one predetermined stance. Things arise from the outer and from the inner. We use whatever is appropriate for the present, whatever the task at hand requires. We take ownership of our effort. All else rests in its place, securely, from our respect for all. The whole circle is available to us, to choose from, to draw upon. The nucleus becomes the pivot, hinging us firmly to its inherent stability.

Enough cannot be said about the centre. It is to be felt and put to use. Being respectful is one way ahead. To reconcile years of obstruction or antagonism may take time. We may begin by being civil.

Civility is not a tense, holding back of hostility. It is openness that leads us to listen. This is of great use, in situations and interaction, at work or at home. If we come up against a problem or opposition, we do not presuppose our attitude or decisions. (Much of anger is assumed. We assume a threat from something or someone and feel angered in advance of knowing the facts.) Our civility frees us from assumptions. It allows us to listen to every point of view, to each side of a situation. If people repeat past complaints, instead of dismissing them, we take further notice. A problem evidently persists, somewhere. We check. If all is clear, that's fine. If it isn't, it comes to light. If it is in our purview of control, we respond. If it is out of our control, we keep it in mind. Our decisions are thus informed and rounded. Each interaction adds to our knowledge—of work or life processes, of others or something about ourselves.

Again, in listening, we are accessible. Others feel they can approach us. Their views will not be disrespected, even if we disagree. If there are divisions between people or groups, we, effortlessly, are in a position to hear opposing voices. As we hear them, we may see that both voices, both ends, however extreme, have reason. In that case, we know that the solution lies somewhere in the middle ground of things, where the truth of both may find space.

In doing so, we are at the centre.

Being civil opens up another facet of the centre. In listening, we are alert to the resource pool at our disposal. We can spot a good suggestion or a way forward offered to us by the people around us. It also reveals the strengths and frailties within us and our team of people, at work or at home. We open ourselves to working with what best we have here and now, rather than being stuck in wishing or lamenting for more. Our leaning is thus constructive—an attribute of the centre.

Importantly for our own selves, being civil keeps the onus on our conduct. It is enough to weaken the pull of other things on us. We watch our form, gently—our tone and manner of expression. That checks us from being brash or unthinking. It prevents us from playing out our own stress onto other things or people and averts unnecessarily complicating a situation.

It can tire us out too, such civility to one and all. At such points, we may stop, momentarily, and allow old patterns to express themselves. But now we can hear the inner voice trashing things, we know what we are doing, and we know the worth of that. Also, if someone else trashes us, we don't necessarily have to engage and get stuck. We recognize that this may be coming from pain and insecurity. We silently offer our understanding and move on.

A popular story from the life of the Buddha tells of a young monk, Sona, who had been a lute player in his previous, worldly avatar. His wish was to find eternal happiness through the ways of the Buddha. The Buddha instructed him to practise mindfulness, especially while walking. The monk, in his eagerness to master the practice, walked back and forth all day long for many days till his feet were filled with sores, and he was in pain. Disappointed and dejected from the result of his practice, he contemplated giving up his monkhood. At this point, the Buddha intervened.

'Tell me, Bhikshu,' the Buddha asked the young monk, 'what would happen if the strings on your lute were too loose?'

'Oh! They wouldn't play any music!' said Sona.

'And were the strings on your instrument too tight, would that play good music?'

'Not at all!' said the monk. 'That would either fashion a very harsh sound, or the strings would snap!'

'Our practice and our lives too, are like your lute,' said the Buddha. 'If we are too loose, then nothing of use will come out of us. And if we are taut and rigid about things, we become unpleasant and harsh, and may break.'

The instruction indicates the middle way, which is not a compromised zone of grey. It is the centre with emphasis on balance.

The centre, by its definition, is away from extremes. Thus, wilfully abandoning the pull of the extremes takes us towards the centre and its balance.

Such balance is not a tight line to walk on. Nor is it another dread-ridden exercise for us to muster great strength to perform. Our bodies function on balance and equilibrium. A constant body temperature and pH factor is the most fundamental evidence of homeostasis—the phenomenon of equilibrium every system works to maintain, within us and in all of nature.

Balance and equilibrium thus *naturally* exist. It is excess that causes strain. When we think too much, or are obsessed with our desires, aspirations or worries, we stretch and strain ourselves to drive the brain and body beyond their innate rhythm.

We don't have to lift or push ourselves up and ahead, in any way, to know balance; rather, we may take several steps back, and drop stuff, if need be—our expectation, our fight (whatever that is), our tense attitude towards the day or anything that is burdensome, here and now. That done, we breathe. In that conscious moment, we are aligned to the centre.

From the centre's balance, we function differently. Nothing is all good or all bad. This is true for us and for our understanding of others.

If a colleague or a family member does something we dislike, we do not dismiss him or her completely. We note what irks us, but also deliberately recall what is positive about the other—a past action, a word of kindness or encouragement, a generous sharing, humour, a talent we respect or any other redeeming quality—anything that comes to mind.

Again, at work, if a task is not executed the way we would prefer it to be, we hold back from dismissing the team or the person's *entire* effort. We consider the big picture as well as the details. From the centre, the micro and macro have equal attention. Nothing is too small to dismiss if done well, nothing is too big to overshadow all else. We pause from painting everything with the same brush. Separating the strands, we see what works here, what doesn't, what is satisfactory or close to it, and what is not. Our approach is level.

Such an approach works to reconcile entire perspectives that seem opposing. If others advocate a particular way, and our truth or milieu pulls us to another extreme, we needn't trash such concern in one stroke. We keep our options open to understand the other's point of view and derive value from it, whenever that may happen. With sensitivity, we select what works for us or appeals to our deeper reason. If that seems impossible, we offer our respect to their truth, at the very least.

The centre thus tempers conflict. It makes our responses stable. Stable emotions allow us to adapt, continuously. Because we aren't consumed by the flux of the extremes within, our attention is accessible for us to do other things.

Stability, here, isn't static and immovable. It does not imply that we hold onto one thing, and stay fixedly there. Stability is a quiet, fluid, *moving* disposition, between the inner and the outer. It is our pleasant commitment to stay at the centre, where all is heard and regarded with value. It is our inclination to find a point of confluence between the extremes, with warm reason. This search for confluence makes us fluid. The centre's constancy comes from balancing the forces to grant both stillness and movement, simultaneously. It is stable and dynamic, together.[53]

The concept of stable balance as fluid and moving was articulated also by Albert Einstein in 1930, in a letter he wrote to his son, Eduard. Einstein's advice was to help his son keep melancholia at bay. He told Eduard that to move on, it was essential to work or keep engaged. 'It is the same with people as it is with riding a bicycle,' he said, and then implied, 'To keep your balance, you must keep moving.'

Again, in the Sanskrit word *dharma*, the concept of stability and movement together, finds expression. Dharma signifies the essence of a thing or a being. It also denotes truth—truth that we arrive at from love for all beings.[54] The word *dharma* means to hold, to bear, from *dhruva*, meaning 'pole'. Thus, *dharma* is an axis, an inner pivot, rooted in truth. It aids the balancing of extremes. It is this that participates in change, by remaining constant.[55]

A stable, fluid balance from inclusivity as an inherent abode, participates in change while remaining centred in the truth.

Participating in the present is onward movement. It reveals our respect for time. We value the present moment and therefore engage with it. This partaking needn't be fraught with anxiety.

'If you are a marathon runner, you have to learn how to pace yourself,' says Buddhist teacher Tenzin Palmo[56], the head of the Dongyu Gatsal Ling Nunnery. 'It's not like you are running a 100-yard sprint! If you have to run for miles and miles, you have to get into a good rhythm, a good pace, so that you can go on without completely collapsing.'

As we move on, the onus to determine the pace we wish to set is up to *us*. However much it seems that work or the world around pushes us to perform at a certain pace, yet from the centre, we recognize that we have a choice at every point. 'I have to do this, I have to have the new stuff, I have to keep up, I have to make it,' is still out of *choice*, whether at work, in indulgence or on social media. We *choose* to want a certain position, which may put us under pressure. We are not pressured by anyone else's desires but our own. We take ownership of that fact. If the burden of our targets is too much to bear and is making us unpleasant in manner and temperament, then perhaps we need to reset our aspirations. Perhaps what we aspire for is not in sync with our current abilities or resources and time frame, and is stressing us out. We may pause, get a sense of our bearings, take stock if possible and then move on.

We may also pause each time we feel an emotion powerfully—grief, anger, pleasure, joy, gratitude or numbness. To sit and breathe for a moment, feeling and observing the full force or power of an emotion, gives it its due. Recognizing it keeps us alive; pausing to observe it allows us depth.

We touch as much depth as that which may not burden us. Our ability to know things deeply is of little point if such depth pulls us under, or interrupts our flow onward. Such is true for our sensitivity as well. If we are super sensitive and take things to heart, our flow is in peril of constant interruption. Thus, we place onus where it is due, for things pleasant or unpleasant, to free ourselves of unnecessary baggage. If someone is appreciative and encouraging, it is to his/her credit for being so; if someone is unkind, it is a reflection on him/her. Nothing in effect can get us to stop and get stuck. We flow on, like moving water.

In our march forward, so that we may not skim the surface or heedlessly brush aside another's concern, there are markers to check for, to know that we are indeed aligned to the centre. One such pointer is our readiness to spot the truth.

Each time we remember a person from whom we have learnt, gained or benefitted, in any measure, we stay close to the truth. It could be recalling an initial recommendation from where our work may have grown, or the source of inspiration, encouragement or constructive critique that spurred us on. It could be a friend who unexpectedly sends across a dish we were longing and wishing for. Each is a medium, pouring in energy into the path of our progress. Placing credit where it is due, keeps us at the centre, in its truth.

Every moment we are truthful or experience a moment of truth, seeing or saying how things really are, whether in our favour or not, we do so from the centre.

On every occasion that we take ownership of our faults—the harshness of our anger, our arrogance or ignorance; and when we admit to, rather than deny or cover up, if and when our loved ones have erred—we function from the centre, from the truth.

Whenever we approach a situation with fairness, with no bias or result in mind, we do so from the centre. The centre comes to be by our admitting to the fact or reality of things, agreeable or distressing, that have transpired in our lives. It is lucid with the truth of our traits and desires. From here, we are alert to the voice of the ego—its need to control, its expectations and its want for attention. When we are fair in approach, we override the ego and its desire to control or expect. Our openness propels us instead from the centre's truth, and back towards it.

Thus, we advance in the practice of truth, empowered in knowing that we can be clear-headed *and* confused, on occasion; that we have been strong and weak, at times. We are aware of the span of strengths and susceptibilities we traverse, as yet. Our participation in the present is alert, because we are capable of contributing *and* destroying, of integrating and disarranging.

The centre's truth keeps us starkly aware of our choices and leanings.

Our courage-humility keeps us steady in approach and observant to the truth. Our respect for time sparks the now and here alive. It propels us to offer our effort to the present.

Engaged, our narrative moves on.

We are hinged to the moving present from within, in fluid equilibrium.

ACKNOWLEDGEMENTS

My thanks and gratitude, first to all those who shared their stories and to all the experts, many of whom are mentioned in this book, for their time and help. Thanks in particular to Dr S.N. Chaudhry of the Vidya Sagar Institute of Mental Health, Neuro & Allied Sciences, for encouraging me to work on this book.

I thank the commissioning team at Rupa Publications for setting a date for me to finish it, and the editorial team for its keen corrections and editing of text. Thank you, Tina Rajan, for the illustrations in the book.

I also thank my friends and colleagues, near and afar, who've wished my work well, and my teachers in school and at university for everything I learnt from them, especially Dr Meenakshi Gopinath, for having led us to learn, share and rejoice, deeply.

And my endless gratitude to family—my dad Amol, my mum Anupama, my brother Nalin and my husband Rajat, for their love and friendship; and to my mum-in-law Sharda and dad-in-law Ravi, for all their care and support.

ENDNOTES

1. A handful of Indian states and certain tribes, such as the Khasis of Meghalaya, are matriarchal or matrilineal. Here, the woman inherits the family property and heads decisions pertaining to the family.
2. 2019, Hindi, Producers: Anurag Kashyap, Nidhi Parmar and Reliance Entertainment.
3. D. Arora and P. Batra, 'Mental Ability, Health and Well-being of Children Belonging to Joint and Nuclear Families', in Radhey Shyam and Azizuddin Khan (eds), *Clinical Child Psychology*, Kalpaz Publications, 2009.
4. Amit Kauts and Balwinder Kaur, *A Study of Children's Behaviour in Relation to Family Environment and Technological Exposure at Pre-Primary Stage*, 2011.
5. Personal communication with Dr Rao over email.
6. S.B. Bansal, Sanjay Dixit, Geeta Shivram, Dhruvendra Pandey and Satish Saroshe, 'A Study to Compare Various Aspects of Members of Joint and Nuclear Family', *Journal of Evolution and Medical Dental Sciences*, Vol. 3, Issue 03, 20 January 2014, pp. 641–48, D01:10:14260/jemds/2014/1879.
7. PTI, 'Arunachal MLA's Son "Beaten to Death" in Delhi, Anger Spills Over,' *The Times of India*, 31 January 2014.
8. Personal conversation with Rishi Talwar.
9. LGBTQ is an initialism that stands for lesbian, gay, bisexual, transgender and queer.
10. Created by Hectic Content.

11 https://www.youtube.com/watch?v=n-jdjR380GY.
12 Personal conversation with Dr Sharma.
13 https://www.youtube.com/watch?v=ktIwY3gqmZc.
14 Reported by Manish Kumar, 'Patna Tops Wi-Fi Use at Railway Stations. Mostly for Porn, Says Official,' NDTV, 19 October 2016, https://www.ndtv.com/india-news/wi-fi-used-most-at-patna-railway-station-mostly-to-watch-pornography-1475214, accessed 11 January 2021.
15 Personal conversation with Dr Jha.
16 Personal communication with Dr Sharma.
17 Interview with Manisha Amin for the film titled *The Subtext of Anger*.
18 Erving Goffman, *Presentation of Self in Everyday Life*, Edinburgh: University of Edinburgh, 1956.
19 Interview with Dr Dougherty for the film titled *The Subtext of Anger*.
20 In 2011, the Institute of Psychiatry, Psychology and Neuroscience at King's College, London, narrowed down a part of Chromosome 3 (called 3p25-26) as a determining region for genes that could be involved in recurrent depression. In 2019, however, researchers at the University of Colorado Boulder quashed claims that any single gene could be responsible for depression. According to them, there are many variants that influence depression. Factors could be genetic and environmental.
21 Interview with Dr Menon for the film titled *The Subtext of Anger*.
22 ibid.
23 Interview with Dr Samuel for the film titled *The Subtext of Anger*.
24 Interview with Dr Dougherty for the film titled *The Subtext of Anger*.
25 Interview with Dr Richardson for the film titled *The Subtext of Anger*.
26 Dean Burnett, *The Idiot Brain*, Guardian Books, 2016, 'Think You're Clever, Do You?' p. 123.

27 Interview with Dr DiGiuseppe for the film titled *The Subtext of Anger*.
28 Interview with Dr Davidson for the film titled *The Subtext of Anger*.
29 Interview with Leonard Berkowitz for the research of the film titled *The Subtext of Anger*.
30 Ramya Patelkhana, 'AIIMS Opens Special Psychiatric OPD for Cyber Addicts,' Newsbytes, 26 October 2016.
31 Interview with Dr Chattarji for the research of the film titled *The Subtext of Anger*.
32 'The Quiet Brain of the Athlete', *New York Times*, 18 December 2019, https://www.nytimes.com/2019/12/18/well/move/sports-athletes-brain-hearing-noise-running.html.
33 Interview with Dr McEwen for the film titled *The Subtext of Anger*.
34 Interview with Tenzin Palmo for the film titled *The Subtext of Anger*.
35 Interview with Dr Davidson for the film titled *The Subtext of Anger*.
36 Interview with Paul Rozin for the film titled *The Subtext of Anger*.
37 Interview with Colin Camerer for the film titled *The Subtext of Anger*.
38 Interview with Professor Nolen-Hoeksema for the film titled *The Subtext of Anger*.
39 Those suffering major to severe depression may require carefully guided intervention for physical activity, in addition to medication and counselling.
40 Indian and Buddhist traditions of mind, amongst others.
41 A person who practices this discipline of discernment, is, in the Indian tradition, a *Jnana Yogi*.
42 Joseph Campbell, *The Hero with a Thousand Faces*, 1949.
43 American journalist and political commentator Bill Moyers in conversation with Joseph Campbell.

44 Lecture by Tenzin Palmo.
45 Interview with Jaggi Vasudev for the research of the film *The Subtext of Anger*.
46 Just as intelligence is not the work of one specific region of the brain, but of many, interlinked regions. (Dean Burnett, *The Idiot Brain*, p. 137).
47 Heinrich Robert Zimmer, *Jainism: Philosophies of India*, edited by Joseph Campbell, 1969.
48 Interview with Dr Powell for the film titled *The Subtext of Anger*.
49 H. Zimrin, *A Profile of Survival, Child Abuse and Neglect*, 1986.
50 Interview with Professor Nolen-Hoeksema for the film titled *The Subtext of Anger*.
51 Interview with Dr Powell for the film titled *The Subtext of Anger*.
52 'Ego' in Sanskrit is *Ahamkaar*. *Aham* = I, *Kaar* = to do, create. Therefore, *Ahamkaar* = all which I have done or created. On the other hand, *Bhu* = to be, *Bhutva* = to become, becoming. There is no action involved and therefore no judgment, no credit or discredit. *Bhutva* is simply to be or to become.
53 The notion is also expressed in the Egyptian concept of time. Neheh is the cycles of time aligned to the sun, while its counterpart Djet, is time which is eternal and complete. It is finished but lives on and so is timeless.
54 Chaturvedi Badrinath, *The Mahabharata: An Inquiry into the Human Condition*, 2007.
55 Steven Rosen, *Essential Hinduism*, 1955.
56 Interview with Tenzin Palmo for the film titled *The Subtext of Anger*.

INDEX

Addictions, 50
Aeronautics engineer, 19
Aggression, 176, 192
Aggression and altruism, 137
All India Institute of Medical Sciences (AIIMS), 138
Alzheimer's disease, 85
Amin, Manisha, 53
Anger, 172
Anger-blame-pain, 186
Anger trajectory, 93
Anxiety, 74, 78
Appearance, 16
Attention, 74
Attraction, 151
Auditory Neuroscience Laboratory, 141
Aversion, 151
Awareness, 77
Awareness and intelligence, 164
Ayurveda, 153

Background experience and expectation, 21
Balance and equilibrium, 196
Belief system, 145
Belly of Whale, 157
Berkowitz, Leonard, 137
Biomedical model, 51
Bio-psycho-social model, 51
Bipolar, 150
Bipolarity, 121, 150, 152, 155, 159
Bipolar pattern, 123
Blame, 102
Body awareness, 144
Buddhist tradition, 162

Calligraphy, 141
Camerer, Colin, 145
Campbell, Joseph, 157
Centre, 196
  shifts, 173
Chain of stores
  mobility/financial freedom, 22–23
Chand, B., 5
Chattarji, Sumantra, 139
Chemical imbalance, 69
Childhood
  associations, 88
  imprints, 87
  memories, 64, 85
Chronic anger-blame, 101
Chronic illness, 78
Circuits of positivity, 176
Civil contractor, 31
Cloudiness and confusion, 143
Cognitive-behavioural approach, 63
Cohesion and harmony, 155

Collective pool, 16
Comfort mechanism, 90
Community, 6, 18
Concentric, 54
Coping mechanisms, 165
Counter movements
   attraction, 151
   aversion, 151
Courage, 173, 175, 181
Crucial links, 108
Cyber addiction, 138

Dark emotion, 163
Darkness, 152, 156
Davidson, Richard, 99, 142
Degree of control, 9
Degree of independence, 14
Degree of indulgence, 14
Dejection-induced depression, 121
Demarcation, 151
Depression, 40, 62, 64, 73, 106, 192
Destructive power, 161
Diagnostic and Statistical Manual of Mental Disorders (DSM-5), 52
Diet, 144
DiGiuseppe, Raymond, 131
Disabling resistance, 106
Disappointment, 75
Dishonesty, 173
Domestic affairs, 14
Dopamine, 69
Dougherty, Darin, 64
Dread-ridden exercise, 196
Dynamism, 178

Eastern traditions, 129

Eccentric, 54
Ecosphere, 21
Education and exposure, 8
Education on sex, 34
Ego, 171, 190
Einstein, Albert, 197
Electric signals, 99, 150
Emotion, 161, 199
Emotional
   associations, 87
   circuits, 21
   disequilibrium, 106
   disorders, 129
   equilibrium, 25
   instability, 172
   memories, 139
   sphere, 149
   stress, 185
Enforced compliance, 18
Enzyme production, 78
Exercise, 141, 144
Expression, 16
External elements, 160

Family
   business, 14
   structure, 15
   wedding, 183
Fatigue sets, 103
Fear, 114, 161
Fear and envy, 160
Fission reaction, 161

Gadget-savvy grandchildren, 19
Gardening, 141
Gay activist, 42
Gender roles, 15
Genetic map, 64
Gere, Richard, 43

Gibbs, Herschelle, 134
Goffman, Erving, 53
Granovette, Mark, 17
Graphics
   images and sounds, 46
   studio, 50
Grief and anger, 130
Gross injustice, 175
Group thinking, 12
Guilt-anger, 84

Habitual pain, 174
Habitual resistance, 167
Harassment, 40
Hardship, 166
Health and wellness, 188
Heterosexuality, 42
Heterosexual
   persons, 40
   relationships, 35
HIV-AIDS awareness event, 43
Homophobic society, 41
Homosexuality, 40
Hostility, 176
Humility, 173, 189

I-consciousness, 190
Identity, 16
Independent expression, 25, 60
Indian anti-obscenity laws, 44
Indian community, 16
Indian culture, 43
Indian metaphysical literature, 156
Indian railways, 46
Indian tradition, 152
Indignation, 18
Inflammation, 109
Information technology
   professional, 25
Infrequent condition, 22
Inherent alignment with movement, 74
Inherent state of equilibrium, 191
Injustice, 155
Innate rhythm, 196
Instant messages, 139
Instant reactions, 139
Internal shift, 159
International shooting champions, 7
Internet addiction disorder (IAD), 139
Intrusion, 80, 83
Involuntary discharge, 186
Irksome enquiry needles, 154
Iyer, Harish, 42
Iyer, Padma, 42

Jha, Mrinal, 49
Joint family, 6, 15, 26
   aunts, 26
   cousins, 26
   grandparents, 26
   uncles, 26

Kraus, Nina, 141

Laboratory of Neuroendocrinology, 141
Learned helplessness, 63
LGBTQ community, 40
Light-hearted exchange, 17
Line of command, 6
Losing control, 30
Low immunity, 144

Madison-Wisconsin University, 133

Manipulation and falsehood, 173
McEwen, Bruce, 141
Measure of humility, 181
Medical experts, 139
Meditation, 143
Melancholia, 72
Menon, Usha, 94, 97
Mental
   emotional health, 20
   construct, 168
   health, 40
Metamorphosis, 158
Model theories, 51
Modern
   techniques, 49
   therapy, 69
Momentary power, 175
Moment of truth, 200
Mood-altering prescription drugs, 69
Mood disorder, 62
Motivations for self-presentation, 53
Mythical stories, 167

National Centre for Biological Sciences, 139
National shooting champions, 7
Neural pathway, 150
Neuronal signals, 77–78
Neurons fire, 77
Neurotransmitters, 69
Newton's Third Law of Motion, 151
New York's laws and law-enforcement officers, 48
Nolen-Hoeksema, Susan, 64, 178
Non-heterosexual persons, 40
Nuclear family, 13, 15, 22

Online advertisement, 42
Oriental antiquity, 152
Overarching philosophy, 166

Painful memories, 115
Palmo, Tenzin, 142, 158
Pandora's box, 75
Parental home, 28
Parking attendant, 138
Past intrusion, 167
Phenomenon of equilibrium, 196
Physical activity, 138
Physical discomfort, 137
   fatigue, 24
   lack of sleep, 24
   nausea, 24
Physical pain, 137
Physiological effects, 62
Physiological equilibrium, 78
Pneumonia, 185
Positive emotions, 167, 185, 186
Positive sensation, 167
Postpartum depression, 24
Powell, Andrew, 171
Pride parade, 42
Process
   of depression, 75
   of education, 176
   of harnessing time and effort, 148
Protesters, 43
Psychomotor skills, 51
Psychotherapists, 146
Public spaces, 47

Rao, Deepali, 12
Repression and suppression, 34
Resistance, 107, 109, 119

Rhythm, 121
Rhythms of mind-psyche-body, 160
Roles, 19
Routine, 148
Routine and resource arrangement of family, 17
Rozin, Paul, 144

Safety, 162
Samuel, Andrew, 97
Self-blame, 75
Self-delusion, 172
Self-image, 90
Semi-precious stones, 5
Sense of positivity, 39
Sense of security, 11
Sense of unity, 185
Sensuality, 43
Serotonin, 69
Sessions of counselling, 60
Sexual abuse, 48
Sexual alliance, 41
Sexual discomfort, 41
Sexual dissatisfaction, 45
Sexuality, 34, 40, 43
Sexual literacy, 46
Sexual maturity and responsibility, 46
Shades of spectrum, 156
Sharma, Pulkit, 45, 52
Shetty, Shilpa, 43
Shvetambar and Digambar, 4
Signals, 108
Sitaram Bhartiya Institute of Science and Research, 59
Sleep, 73, 144
Sleep patterns, 139
Smoking, 51

Smoking hookah, 7
Social-historical-political facts, 68
Social media, 18, 139
Societal normalcy, 45
Spirituality and Psychiatry Special Interest Group of Royal College of Psychiatry, 186
Sport, 141
Stability, 197, 198
Stable emotions, 197
Statistical model, 49
Stillness and movement, 197
Stimulation, 140
Substance abuse, 115

Talwar, Rishi, 40, 140
Tata Docomo, 45
Therapy sessions, 82
'The Strength of Weak Ties,' 17
Thought-memory-impulse, 76
Tomar, Chandro, 6
Tomar, Prakashi, 6
Traditional attire, 27
Transformation, 158, 162
Transformative power of darkness, 158
Trauma, 41

Unprogressive family, 26
Urban metropolises, 20
Urinary tract infection, 85

Vasudev, Jaggi, 162
Videos of sexual abuse and assault, 46
VIMHANS (Vidyasagar Institute of Mental Health, Neuro & Allied Sciences), 49
Violence, 16

Vital energy, 103
Vital organs and systems, 100

Weakness, 144
Weak ties, 18
Well-founded action, 155
Wheel
  of acute despair, 38
  of anger and guilt, 63
  of injustice, 176
Whirlpool of despair, 105

Wholeness, 55
Wi-Fi, 46
Wiring up associations, 154
Wisdom, 167
Witnessed aggression, 53
Woman
  financial freedom, 22-23
  mobility freedom, 22-23
  professionals, 20
  sensuality, 44